Isle of Tatsu

Sometimes danger follows you home.

SUSAN FOUST

ISBN: 978-1-09835-553-1 Print

ISBN: 978-1-09835-554-8 eBook

This book is dedicated to my children: Paul and Sara. My heartfelt thanks for your love and encouragement.

And for Liam – my favorite reader.

CONTENTS

Isle of Tatsu

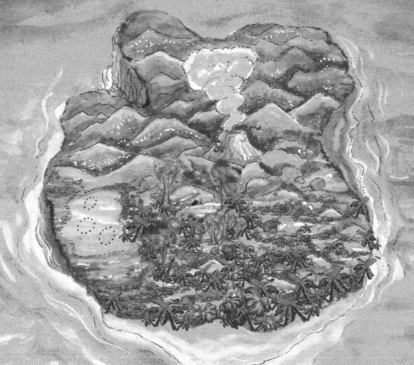

Map Legend

- Komodo Burrows
- Volcano
- Cave
- Waterfall

Prologue

Matt could feel the bone-jarring vibration of the Bell helicopter through his seat as he struggled to get comfortable. They had left Darwin, Australia, a little after daybreak, and the early morning sun was already bouncing off the sparkling waters of the Timor Sea.

Matt was seated beside his older brother, Sam, in the back of the chopper while their dad sat up front with the pilot. During the flight plan briefing with Captain Andrews, Bob Sawyer had given the pilot the geographic coordinates of the island that had almost taken the lives of his two sons a couple of months ago.

Matt shifted in his seat, trying to relax. The scaly, reptilian skin on his chest was starting to itch again, even though his mother had put lots of ointment under his shirt. But that wasn't the worst of his problems. Looking at the top of his right foot, Matt wiggled his small toe. He could feel it growing, taking over his toenail, wanting nothing more than to rip through the tough leather of the boot and tear something to shreds.

The island appeared suddenly, its profile low against the horizon. Misty, gray clouds hung over it, making it appear deserted and foreboding. The pilot sighted the island and turned toward a sandy spit of land, descending expertly on the narrow beach. Matt stared at the back of Andrews' helmet. *You really want to know why we came back? Apparently, this place isn't finished with me and my brother yet.*

It's looking to reclaim one of its own.

Chapter 1

THE VOYAGE BEGINS

If Matt Sawyer had known what the coming week had in store for him and his older brother, he would have stayed in bed that morning. But instead, he opened sleepy eyes and looked at the clock on his bedside table. He beat the alarm by sixteen minutes! *Perfect*, he thought. *An even number.* Grinning, he pushed the off button, and swung his legs to the floor.

Matt dressed quickly and couldn't resist the urge to check his backpack again. His tightly rolled clothes and toiletries in plastic bags fit together like pieces of a jigsaw puzzle. Everything was packed: check. Matt's water-resistant watch was on his wrist and sunglasses hung around his neck on a rubber lanyard. Neither he nor his brother, Sam, were taking any electronic devices. Sailing on the open sea was a real-life adventure that was more thrilling than any video game they owned.

Matt looked around his room to make sure he wasn't leaving a giant mess behind. After making his bed, he straightened the books on his desk so that the edges were neatly aligned. He walked over to a large terrarium near the window, twisted off the top of a glass jar filled with chopped up fruits and vegetables from last night's dinner, and dropped in a handful of food. Matt watched as his bearded dragon began inching down the branch toward breakfast, lunch, and dinner.

His Uncle Paul had given him the reptile a couple of months ago, and Matt really enjoyed having it around. He tapped on the glass to get its attention and laughed when the dragon ignored him. "See ya, Pickles, I'll be back in a couple of days," Matt said.

He hoped his mother would remember to feed his pet while he was gone. As he put the jar down, it knocked over a family picture taken last winter when Matt had celebrated his tenth birthday. They had sailed to nearby Dundee Beach and spent three days fishing and mud crabbing. His mum had snapped a couple of photos of them being silly on the deck of their sailboat and this was Matt's favorite one. His older brother by four years, Sam, pretended to walk the plank while Captain Matt balanced a fake parrot on his shoulder. Impulsively, he slipped the picture into a zippered side pocket, then went downstairs to join his family.

Matt and Sam live with their parents in Darwin, Australia, or "paradise on earth," as their mum is so fond of saying. When planning their trip, the family decided that early July would be the best time because the days were warm, and the nights pleasantly cool. And most of the rainy season was over, which meant fewer storms on the ocean.

The Sawyer family had purchased their forty-foot sailboat when Matt was five years old, and he felt as comfortable on the water as he did on land. It slept four people comfortably, and they enjoyed taking her out for day trips or week-long excursions along the western coast of Australia. It was also equipped for blue water sailing if they wanted to venture into the ocean for longer distances.

This time it would just be Matt and Sam on board, but Bob and Sarah Sawyer knew their sons were up to the challenge. Sam had been involved in the local chapter of the Australian Naval Cadets since he was twelve years old and was knowledgeable about sailing fundamentals, navigation, and safety on the water.

Matt joined his mum in the kitchen and helped her pack their food and provisions in lightweight plastic totes, putting the heavier things on the bottom.

"Matt, there is plenty of food here," his mother said. "A jar of Vegemite, soups, canned foods, your favorite Tim Tams, and lots more. I baked the bread yesterday, so it will be fresh for a couple of days. And, oh, here's some homemade granola bars for your brekky at sea."

"Mum, you're the best." Matt gave her a hug and held on longer than usual. He knew she was worried about Sam and him sailing alone and she probably wouldn't relax until they returned home several days from now.

Sam and Dad were in the dining room going over last-minute instructions. Sam folded a navigation map and tucked it in a waterproof satchel. "Okay, I think that's everything," Dad said. "Let's head over to the marina and get this show on the road."

Ten minutes later they arrived at Shorty's Marina, where their sail-boat, *Zephyr*, was waiting for them, bobbing gently in the water. Matt and his mum put away the supplies in the galley while Dad and Sam did a thorough check of the navigation and communication systems.

It was finally time to shove off, and Mum and Dad gave them both hugs and wishes for a safe journey. Luke, their Australian Shepherd, was trying to get their attention by jumping up and barking. Matt laughed and buried his face in the dog's soft fur.

"Bye, Luke. Take care of things while we're gone, boy. Maybe next time you can come with us."

A challenging maneuver for any boat is leaving the dock, so Sam listened carefully to his dad's advice about wind direction and strength.

"Sam, the wind is pushing starboard side, bow out, so remember to reverse the engine and use the left rudder to pivot into the wind," Dad shouted. He then removed the dock lines after the boat had cleared the pier and tossed them onto the wooden walkway. They were off!

Sarah turned to her husband. "Do you still think this is a good idea?"

"Yes, I do. Sailing is a great way for them to reconnect with each other. Don't worry."

Bob and Sarah smiled and waved until both boys turned their attention to the task of sailing through the light traffic in the marina and heading toward the open sea. Something glinted on the wooden planks, and Sarah bent over to pick it up.

"Look, Bob, it's Sam's St. Christopher medal. He never takes this off, and I know he's going to be upset when he realizes that it's missing."

Wordlessly, Bob held his hand out and Sarah dropped the medal and chain in it. She tried to shake off the sudden feeling of foreboding that swept over her. Luke watched as *Zephyr* became a small blur on the water and whimpered softly.

Chapter 2
OPEN SEA

"Look, Matt!" shouted Sam as he gestured to the Tiwi Islands on starboard side. They had gone there on a fishing safari last year and the highlight of the trip was grilling mouth-watering barramundi on the barby. Lots of tourists visit these islands, but one of their dad's closest friends was a fishing guide there, and he had shared some secluded spots where it was just them and the biting fish.

Matt grinned and gave his brother a thumbs up. He felt exhilarated with the sea spray whipping his face and hair as he and Sam tacked *Zephyr* into the wind. Tacking put the boat on a zigzag course so that the wind changed from one side of the boat to the other. It was an important seamanship skill and required lots of practice.

The Sawyers had customized their sailboat so that it was comfortable for their family of four, and safe for sea cruising. It had a couple of sails: the mainsail and headsail, or jib, which were attached to a moving horizontal piece called the boom.

When they bought the boat, its hull was a dark blue that trapped heat and was faded in spots, so they repainted it a glossy white. The next project was applying coats of lacquer to the vintage teakwood on the deck so that it would repel water, fungi, and insects. Its sleeping quarters were a double berth at the larger end of the boat, a smaller one at forward, and a spacious sleeping space in the galley when the eating benches were folded away.

Toward the end of the afternoon, they were tired but satisfied with the first day of their journey. Matt had dropped some fishing lines in the water early afternoon and caught several good-sized wahoos, which were tossed in an Esky cooler.

As they cleaned up their fishing gear, Sam realized that his St. Christopher medal wasn't hanging around his neck. "Hey, Matt, have you seen my St. Chris anywhere? I guess I snagged the chain on something because it's missing."

"I haven't seen it, but I'll help you look for it," replied Matt. He turned over deck chair cushions, peered inside the cooler, and went through all the food crates they had brought from home. Matt opened the package of Tim Tams and couldn't resist shoving one in his mouth.

"Were you wearing it at the marina?" Matt asked as he rejoined Sam on the deck.

"I haven't taken it off since Granny Sawyer gave it to me two years ago, so, yeah, I was wearing it at the marina," replied Sam sarcastically.

"No need to be salty. Want me to look some more in the galley?" Matt asked.

"No, it'll probably turn up when I need it the most," replied Sam. "Thanks for helping me look, little bro. I'm starving so let's get those fish ready for the barby. Why don't you get started while I check the weather forecast?"

Sam went into the cockpit and listened to the weather radio. He was trying not to worry about the lost medal, but the truth was he felt vulnerable without his lucky talisman.

Matt attached the grill to an outside railing of the boat and lit the charcoal briquettes while Sam cleaned and fileted the wahoo, saving the guts for fishing bait. They tossed the fish on the barby and watched as their dinner sizzled, sending smoke signals into the air.

"My mouth's watering, mate," Sam laughed. "Remember that time Dad was grilling hamburger patties and that huge wave blew up and swamped our dinner?"

"Yeah, it was cold sandwiches that night," Matt grinned.

They roasted sliced veggies from their garden at home and tore off hunks of Mum's sourdough bread to complete their meal. All they needed was the star of the show.

"Five more minutes and this fish is going to melt in your mouth," promised Sam.

Balancing their overflowing plates, they sat down to enjoy their meal with a symphony of bird sounds in the background. Overhead, seagulls shrieked as they circled and dived looking for leftovers.

"You won't get anything here, birds!" Sam yelled. "We licked our plates clean!"

"It's your turn to tidy up, Matt. I'm going to use the satellite phone to check in with Dad."

Matt took the dishes down to the galley and had everything washed and put away in no time. He lined up the utensils in the pull-out drawers but resisted the urge to count them. Matt loved numbers, especially even numbers. His mum said that he was curious about numbers at an early age, counting forward and backward to twenty before he was two years old. And up until a couple of years ago, Matt would count as he walked, always starting off with the left foot as "one." But as he got older, Matt realized that everything didn't need to be counted and sorted. *Numbers are cool, but I'm in control here*, Matt thought as he wiped the countertops.

He looked around the kitchen area as he worked. It was a small but cheery space and had everything they needed to prepare all their meals. They usually ate on the deck, but the galley had a table and two benches that came in handy when the weather wasn't hospitable. Mum had covered the bench cushions with a red, white, and blue nautical fabric that looked great except for a faded area where Matt had thrown up after getting seasick. It was covered with a round pillow, and affectionately referred to as "Matt's Spot."

The oven, fridge, and sink were close together, which helped with food prep and cooking, especially in running seas. Dad surprised Mum with an electric rice cooker last Christmas, and it quickly became one of the most used appliances in the galley. A speedy stir fry with shrimp or fish was an ace dinner that everyone enjoyed.

Matt joined his brother who was stretched out on the comfy deck and they watched as stars blinked on, one by one, in the evening sky.

"Stars always look much brighter over the ocean," said Sam in a quiet voice. He pointed out the Southern Cross constellation, which is only seen in the southern hemisphere. Its shape is defined by five stars, the bottom two pointing toward polar south.

Matt finally spoke. "It's kind of weird not having our parents here, but I'm glad it's just us, Sam." He looked over at his big brother for reassurance.

"I'm glad too, Matt. It's going to be a great trip for sure," replied Sam.

The Sawyer family did lots of nighttime sailing and followed all the safety rules. As soon as the sun went down, Sam switched on the stern's white light to let other boaters know that they were stationary. If *Zephyr* had been underway, they would have turned on a green starboard light and a red one on the port side. The mast was also lit by a white light that had to be visible from two miles away.

Dad and Sam had drawn up a watch duty schedule so there would always be someone awake and alert in the cockpit. Since Sam was older and more experienced, he would be responsible for most of it, but Matt would share the duty a couple of hours before dawn.

The *Zephyr* also used AIS (automatic identification system) which is a VHF radio-based transponder device that would prevent their boat from being in a collision with another vessel.

"I'm taking the first watch, so go get some sleep," Sam ordered as he strapped on the red LED headlamp that let him monitor the instruments on the console without harming his night vision.

Matt gave one final look at the stars winking in their nighttime playground, then went below to the smallest bedroom on the boat. It had always been his favorite because it reminded him of a cozy tree house, with its walls and roof only an arm's length away. He opened the dual portholes and breathed in the bracing, salty air. Matt was completely knackered and was fast asleep within minutes.

Chapter 3

STORM

The brothers spent the next two days sailing in great conditions, enjoying postcard perfect weather. *Zephyr* had the wind at her back, and they were sailing over eighty nautical miles a day. Sam didn't even seem to mind that Matt caught more fish than him. But that all changed on the evening of the third day at sea.

The midnight watch started quietly enough, but after an hour, Sam saw lightning flashes three to four nautical miles away on the horizon. The wind had picked up and he could see heavy clouds flitting over the brightness of the full moon, which puzzled him because the weather forecast had predicted clear skies and calm seas.

Sam checked various instruments in the cockpit and was concerned when he noted a drop in barometric pressure and an increase in wind strength and direction. These two things meant that a storm front was approaching from the southeast. Currently the winds were blowing at twenty-two knots, and the waves were forming foamy crests with lots of spray.

Sam consulted the faded, salt-stained poster on the wall showing the widely used Beaufort Scale, which measured the intensity of weather according to wind power. The scale progressed from calm wind and seas at Level 0 all the way to hurricane conditions at Level 12, and Sam estimated they were currently around a 6 on the Beaufort. Should they run for cover and get out of the storm's path, or would they be forced to ride it out?

Sam automatically reached for his St. Christopher medal to give it a rub for good luck before he remembered that it was still missing. He felt beads of sweat pop out on his forehead as he realized that it would be impossible to outrun this gale.

Sam decided to wake his brother around 1:30 a.m. "Matt, get up! The weather has taken a turn for the worst, and I need you on deck." He tossed him an inflatable safety harness and quickly climbed the ladder topside.

Matt rubbed the sleep out of his eyes, secured the personal flotation device, and joined Sam on deck. The waves were at least fourteen feet high, and the wind was ferocious as it whipped against the sails.

"I thought you said the weather looked fine," Matt shouted to be heard over the storm.

"That's what the early forecast said," Sam yelled back. "This storm blew up really fast! Clip your harness tether to a jackline so you can help with the sails." Jacklines are ropes that run the length of the sailboat from bow to stern and being secured to them reduces your chances of being tossed overboard during rough seas.

The rain and gale force winds lashed at them, making it difficult to see beyond their boat, which seemed ridiculously small in the tempest. The dark seas were lit up by jagged flashes of lightning, which were getting closer and closer.

"Help me reef the mainsail! I'll grab the sail and you take the helm. Hold it as steady as you can," shouted Sam as he lowered the sail and tied the excess to the boom. This reduced the sail area, so less wind was blowing against it.

"Will this work, Sam? We should have reefed before the wind got so bad."

"I told you this storm blew in with no warning," yelled Sam over his shoulder.

Sam and Matt had practiced the technique of shortening the sails back at the marina and in calm seas, under the watchful direction of their dad. And when the family was caught in a sudden thunderstorm last summer, they reefed the sails before the winds became too gusty and their boat easily rode out the storm.

Matt didn't know which was worse: seeing the colossal waves crashing over them when lightning lit up the sky or trying to maintain his footing in darkness not knowing how bad the conditions were. He felt saltwater burning his eyes and pushed wet and matted hair off his forehead for what seemed to be the thousandth time. His muscles were quivering and aching from the effort of standing upright on the slippery deck.

Suddenly an electrical charge crackled the air around the brothers and within seconds, their senses were overwhelmed by a boom of thunder and super-charged lightning flash. Millions of volts lit up everything like an exploding star—illuminating the boat, water, and sky so brightly they had to look away. The mast glowed an eerie blue and the air tasted like burnt marshmallows.

Sam covered his eyes and waited for the ringing in his ears to stop. He had no way of knowing how long this storm would last or if they could ride it out without *Zephyr* taking on more water or capsizing. He waved his arms overhead to get Matt's attention.

"We're going to heave-to. Sheet in the jib to pull it in close. I'll give the winch a couple of turns," Sam shouted the instructions to his brother and stayed close in case Matt needed him at the sail.

After the sail was sheeted, they worked together to tack the boat into the wind, which put it on starboard tack with the headsail facing the wind. Sam turned the steering wheel all the way to windward and locked it, then pushed the tiller toward the mainsail, securing it in that position.

Heaving-to is an effective way to ride out a powerful storm because the boat's helm and sail positions are fixed, which reduces the motion of the waves. It's like parking your boat at sea, which creates a much safer situation onboard.

"Hey, great job, mate," Sam gave his brother a high five. "I'm going to drop the sea anchor too, just to be on the safe side." Standing at the stern, Sam released the drogue which acted like a canvas parachute in the water, slowing their progress even more.

Another hour passed, and the wind and ocean grew calmer. Sam checked the radio and navigation systems, and found to his dismay that they weren't functional, probably due to the lightning strike. The engine's batteries were knocked out as well, which meant they had to rely on wind power. All their communication devices were totally inoperable, including the satellite phone, which got saturated when water had swamped the cockpit area.

This was a serious problem because now they had no way to contact their parents or marine rescue if their boat showed significant damage and they were unable to sail home. Sam decided to not share his concerns with Matt right away; hopefully, a new day would restore power to their instruments.

As the sun rose over the horizon, the ocean was peaceful and still. The storm had left as quickly as it had mysteriously appeared.

"What a bizarre storm," Sam stated, taking a long drink of bottled water. "Did you notice the greenish color of the sky, Matt?"

"Yeah, crazy. Why was that ball of fire sitting on top of our mast?!"

"I'm pretty sure that was St. Elmo's fire," Sam explained. "It's plasma and gases that are created by an electrical charge during a thunderstorm. This is the first time I've experienced it, though. You know, they say that sailors back in the olden days thought St. Elmo's fire was a good luck omen because it meant they were being watched over."

"Well, I guess we were being watched over too, because *Zephyr* held together and we weren't tossed in the sea," Matt said. "Everything turned out okay, right?"

Sam was quiet as he gazed out over the port side. He had an uneasy feeling that their trip had just taken a detour into the unknown, and they were no longer in control.

As the sun rose higher over the calm water, the sea mist began to lift, and they could see the outline of a small island.

Chapter 4

THE ISLAND

"Well, the most important thing we're doing today is figuring out our location using the sextant, but we have to wait until noon when the sun is directly overhead. Matt, how about you dive under the boat and check out the rudder and keel for damage," suggested Sam as he mopped up water from the deck.

Matt stripped down to his bathing trunks and spit on the inside of his goggles for better vision before backflipping off the railing and disappearing under *Zephyr*. When he surfaced, Sam pulled him on board.

"The rudder is bent where it connects to the tiller. The propeller looks okay, and there aren't any cracks or holes in the hull. The radio antennae on the mast is cactus, though. So, basically, we have no way to call Dad, and no one can contact us either." Matt was breathing hard and flung his head from side to side to get the water out of his ears.

"It's true that we're in radio silence out here, but hopefully not for long. I'm more concerned that we have less than two days of fresh water on board. Right now, let's focus on fixing the tiller and see," Sam gestured to the island, "if our neighbor has any water and fruit to share."

Matt looked at the island. It reminded him of a house that had its windows and doors shuttered tightly but you knew someone was home, watching from behind a drawn curtain.

An hour before noon, Sam went to the cockpit and came back with the supplies he needed to take a celestial reading. He opened a worn, leather case, and pulled out a complicated looking instrument and a copy of the *Nautical Almanac*, a yearbook containing astronomical data used by sailors for navigation purposes.

"Matt, this is a sextant and has been used by sailors since the 1700s to help them figure out their location while at sea. The technology still works if I can remember the steps." Sam pointed out the different parts of the instrument such as the two mirrors, the curved arm, and the eyepiece.

Sam had made lots of good friends in the Naval Cadets organization and learned useful skills in the areas of navigation, first aid, and maritime history. One of his favorite classes was learning about older instruments such as sextants and astrolabes.

Matt spoke up. "So, latitude and longitude show where we are on land or water?"

"Yep. Latitude are parallel lines that start at the equator, which is 0 degrees, and measure if your location is north or south. Longitude lines are called meridians and begin at Greenwich, England, which is 0 degrees. These measure east and west positions. So, it looks like the Earth is covered by a grid of lines going up and down, and side to side."

"We're going to use the sextant to get a reading which will accurately measure the angle between the Sun and the Earth's horizon. Even though we all rely on GPS now, it's important to understand the science of basic navigation. All ships and boats are required to carry sextants and have access to the tables of the *Nautical Almanac* as well as having trained officers on board."

Sam talked as he placed everything on the bench below the deck railing. "I wish I had a more accurate timepiece, like a chronometer, but I'll make do with my basic watch. Hold this piece of paper and pencil so they don't blow away."

"I'm going to get several readings of the sun's angle as it ascends, is at the highest point, and as it descends so we have all the numbers to figure out latitude and longitude," Sam informed Matt, as he trained the sextant toward the sun. "I'm putting the sunshade in place, so my eyes are protected. Thank goodness it's not cloudy."

Sam talked out loud as he went through the steps. When he measured the angle of the sun at its highest point, he told Matt that it looked like the sun was sitting directly on the horizon. He then read off the degree measurement numbers on the index arm and micrometer knob, and Matt wrote them down. They recorded the time when they made these sightings, and then consulted the *Nautical Almanac.*

"Wow look at all the numbers in this book! Do they make sense to you?" asked Matt as he turned a couple of the pages.

Sam grinned. "Yeah, that's what I'm learning as a cadet." He used the tables in the *Almanac* to adjust the data, and just like that, he had their geographical coordinates.

"Matt, our latitude is 10° 39' 27" South, and our longitude is 129° 12' 31" East."

The brothers stood at the railing of the boat and gazed at the small isle. They saw a narrow sandy beach, dotted with large and small rocks, which led uphill to dense, tropical foliage. Lazy wisps of gray smoke curled around a summit that rose from the center of the mysterious island.

Chapter 5

DANGER LURKING

"Hey, Matt, do you want to swim over there to that floating rock or lower the dinghy?"

"Let's swim. Heck, I'll race you!" Matt yelled, diving into the water, and getting a head start. He swam hard, lungs burning, but Sam overtook him with a quick burst of speed as they neared the beach.

Sunlight warmed the sand and lit up the many tidal pools that dotted the shore. Dozens of seashells lay scattered around. It looked like any other beach they had ever been on, except that this place was uninhabited and possibly hostile.

The brothers looked toward the dark, unwelcoming trees and trudged toward them, their swim shoes sinking in the sand with every step. *Squelch, squelch.* The contrast between the beach and tropical jungle was clear; like day resisting the pull of night as sunlight struggled to penetrate the thick foliage.

"We're not going too deep in this jungle. I just don't have a good feeling about this place," Sam said as he looked around slowly.

Nope, Matt didn't either. Hopefully, his brother didn't notice the goosebumps on his arms as he rubbed them briskly.

Sam took the lead as they stepped into the trees. The temperature was noticeably cooler than on the beach and the air felt moist and heavy.

Damp leaves brushed against them as they pushed their way through the thick undergrowth, tripping occasionally over gnarled, exposed tree roots. There was an unpleasant smell of decaying and rotting vegetation which hung in the air and wriggled its way inside their noses.

"Do you hear anything, Sam?" asked Matt as he slapped at hungry mosquitos that were dive-bombing his arms and legs.

"Nope. I was just wondering about that, bro. Something's not quite right."

It was eerily quiet. No birds chirping or screeching monkeys. They didn't even hear the high-pitched whine of the relentless mosquitoes, even though they could see them. By the time they swatted them away, the insects had already feasted.

Sam picked up several mangoes lying on the ground, dropping them into a mesh bag attached to his belt that also sheathed a sharp knife. They weren't ripe yet but would be a delicious snack in a couple of days.

"I'm hoping there is a clean water supply close by, but if we don't locate it quickly, we'll just stretch out what we have," said Sam as they continued moving uphill.

The brothers hiked all the way up the western slope until they finally stepped out of the suffocating jungle and took deep, cleansing breaths. They were standing at the base of the volcano that towered over everything on the island. Its steep sides were littered with lots of loose stones and lacey, dried pumice, reminders of past eruptions and pyroclastic flows.

"I've never been this close to a volcano before, and it's a little scary," Sam admitted.

"Is it still active?" Matt asked, picking up one of the volcanic rocks scattered on the ground. It was shiny and black, probably obsidian, and he put it inside his pocket, thinking it would look cool beside his lava lamp at home.

"I think so, because we saw smoke rising from the summit—technically, it's not smoke, but rather a mix of water vapor and different gases—and notice that rotten egg smell? That comes from hydrogen sulfide gas."

Sam kicked at loose pebbles with the toe of his shoe. "We're on a mission for fresh water, so let's say goodbye to this hot rock."

They took a different route down and stumbled into a lush tropical glade, complete with a waterfall spilling into a crystalline pool. Sunlight poured into the small clearing, warming the ground and water. It would be the perfect place to stretch out for a nap with the cascading water sounds in the background.

Sam and Matt filled their canteens with water, dropped in a couple of purification tablets, and drank until their thirst was quenched. They filled several collapsible bottles to take back with them to the boat.

Matt was excited by the discovery of a cave behind the waterfall but backed away from the opening after Sam's warning.

"I wouldn't get too close to that cave, Matt. It's probably home to bats, spiders, and snakes. Or maybe something bigger and more dangerous."

They were leaving the peaceful little glade when they noticed the skeletal remains of an animal, piled under a kapok tree. A beautiful orchid plant grew at the base of the tree as if in loving tribute to whatever animal spent its final day there.

"What kind of animal do you think this was, Sam?"

"No idea. I'm no expert on skeletons, but I guess it could have been a pig or deer." He stood and wiped his grimy hands on his shorts. "C'mon, it's time to go."

They walked briskly through the jungle, swatting at the relent-less mosquitos, until they reached the beach. Suddenly Sam stopped so abruptly that Matt almost ran into the back of him. Right in front of them were some very unusual tracks in the sand.

"I bet a giant crocodile made these," Matt bent down to look closely. It looked like the animal had clawed feet and a huge tail. Australia was home to these dangerous reptiles, and they knew to give a wide berth to these "salties."

"Maybe, so we need to get off this beach before we have a close encounter with it," said Sam as he looked up and down the shoreline. Both boys sprinted across the sand toward the ocean, sidestepping the tangled nests of seaweed that the incoming tide was depositing on the beach. The cool water felt refreshing after the hot stickiness of the island, and Sam let Matt take the lead on the brief swim to their boat.

After they climbed aboard, Matt went looking for a snack in the galley and Sam grabbed the binoculars from the cabin. Leaning against the railing on the port side, he raised the field glasses to his eyes and surveyed the island carefully, paying close attention to the tree line. Sam's patience was rewarded when he saw movement near the rocky end of the beach.

A large, lumbering animal emerged from the jungle, holding its head high and sniffing the air. He couldn't see the entire creature because it crouched behind a boulder. *It's probably a crocodile*, thought Sam as he lowered the binoculars. But saltwater crocodiles can be as long as four meters (around twelve feet) and this animal's tracks didn't indicate an animal of that size. It looked shorter, but more powerful.

Matt watched Sam hang the binoculars on a mast hook and tossed him a banana. "Did you see anything?"

"I was curious about those animal tracks we saw earlier, but no, I didn't see anything moving around. Let's dry out these deck cushions then grab dinner before the sun sets, alright? Maybe a Vegemite sandwich and fruit, since our power is still out," Sam suggested.

"Yeah, sounds good. I hope we can get *Zephyr* ready to sail. Being out here in woop woop isn't my idea of a fun time," Matt replied.

"Well, I don't want to sail at night without power for lights and navigation, so unless it comes back on, we're stuck here until dawn," Sam said. He ducked back into the cockpit to check the instruments again but was disappointed to see that nothing had powered up.

Sam didn't want to alarm his younger brother about possible danger on the island, but when he spied the mysterious animal through the binoculars, the hair on the back of his neck stood up and his mouth went dry. Sam knew this was his primitive "lizard brain" letting him know that danger was near. He told himself that if they stayed on the boat, they were safe, but he wouldn't be able to relax until they pushed off at first light.

This was the first time he and Matt had sailed without their parents, and even though he felt comfortable being in charge, Sam wished his dad were here.

Chapter 6

A MOTHER KNOWS

Bob Sawyer found Sarah sitting on the edge of Matt's bed. "I was look-ing for you all over the house. What are you doing in here?" Bob asked his wife.

"Something has happened to our boys. I feel it in my gut," Sarah's voice trembled. "They are supposed to check in every evening, and we haven't heard from them in over thirty-six hours. And you know how respon-sible Sam is about stuff like that."

"I have to admit, I am concerned that they haven't been in touch. I just called a good friend at Maritime Rescue—Frank Francis—and told him that Sam had missed a check-in with us. He said he wasn't aware of any storm activity in that part of the Timor Sea or had any reports of dis-abled boats, but he would call if he heard anything," said Bob.

"Good. I'm glad you contacted Frank," murmured Sarah. "You know, Matt and Sam are so different from each other, and the older they get, the farther apart they seem. Sam was so protective of Matt when he was younger."

Bob chuckled. "Remember when Matt found that training device that we used on Luke, and he carried it everywhere marking each foot-step with that annoying *click* sound?! And then, unbeknownst to us, Matt took it to school, and several kids made fun of him. Somehow Sam found out about it, resolved the bullying, and convinced Matt to leave the clicker at home."

"Matt has made great progress with his therapist in the past couple of years learning how to manage these behaviors, plus he's doing better socially too. I just want Matt to see himself the way we see him: smart, funny, and caring," Sarah stated.

"Matt needs to step out of his comfort zone a little, and that's the main reason we agreed to let them take this sailing trip. And Sam *is* protective of Matt, so you can rest assured that he'll guard his little brother with his life if necessary. Stop worrying, Sarah. You'll feel better when they contact us today," promised Bob.

"I'll feel better once they are home," said Sarah. "I wish I could shake this nagging feeling that all is not well." She stood up and smoothed the wrinkles from the quilt where she had been sitting. "Let's go downstairs and try to call them again."

Luke nosed open the door to Matt's bedroom. He strolled around the room, paused to look at the bearded dragon in the terrarium, his breath fogging up the glass, then jumped up on the bed and made himself comfortable. *This is a good place to wait*, he thought.

Chapter 7

THE **ATTACK (MATT)**

Matt's watch duty was almost over when he peeked out of the cockpit and saw Sam fast asleep. He knew the plan was to shove off around daybreak, so he only had about twenty minutes to get to the island and then back to the boat before his brother woke up. Matt promised his mum he'd bring her something special and he knew she would like a bloom from the orchid plant they had seen near the waterfall yesterday.

He looked at the island, still undecided about whether to risk a solo visit just for a pretty flower. *Man up, Sawyer*, thought Matt. *What could possibly happen?*

Matt quietly lowered himself into the sea, using the ladder attached to the side of the boat. The swim took less than ten minutes, and he was only slightly winded when he reached the narrow strip of beach. There was scarcely enough light to see where he was going, but Matt was able to get his bearings by sighting the high cliffs that loomed over the island. The worst part was navigating the overgrown jungle trail that was barely wide enough for one person and competing with palm leaves as large as his head in the narrow space.

Arriving at the kapok tree, he walked over to the orchid plant, pulled off the biggest bloom, and hooked it under his swimsuit waistband. *Mum is going to love it*, Matt thought excitedly.

Hearing a rustle in the tree made him look up and he saw a lizard stretched out on the lowest branch. It was almost as long as his arm and was covered with colorful bands and spots arranged in patterns. It looked nothing like the bearded dragon in his terrarium at home.

"Thanks for the flower. See ya," Matt said and took off at a jog.

Matt pretended he was racing the rising sun, crashing through the jungle, but what he saw when he got to the beach stopped him dead in his tracks.

An enormous creature stood between Matt and the water. At first glance it looked like a crocodile—there are plenty of those in Australia—but a closer look revealed a vastly different reptile. Its long, yellow tongue, forked on one end like a snake, flicked in and out, picking up scents. It must have detected the smell of human, because its head swiveled until it was facing Matt. The reptile only had one working eye; the other one, damaged and useless, was covered by thick, puckered scar tissue. This creature was battle-hardened and dangerous.

The gigantic lizard was around three meters (nine feet) in length and had short, bowed legs. Its tail was long and muscular, and rested on the sand like a weapon waiting to be used. The top of its head was unusually flat, leading down to a tapered snout. Sunlight glinted off the grayish color of the skin, which was covered in armor-like scales. But the scariest thing about this reptile were the rows of sharp teeth topped with serrated edges that meant business.

Matt was positive that he was face to face with a Komodo dragon. They're the largest lizards in the world and are the apex predators in their habitat. It didn't seem that interested in him, because it stretched out on the beach and wriggled back and forth in the damp sand.

Matt squatted on the sand, trying to make himself look as small as possible. His thoughts were racing like crazy. *How will I get back to the boat now? If I screamed for help, would Sam hear? If I did scream, is it the last thing I will ever do?*

Quietly, he retreated into the refuge of the trees. Matt decided to return to the glade, then hike down to the rocky beach at the northern end. The swim would be a little longer, but he was okay with that.

Stopping to drink from the waterfall pool, Matt watched the tree lizard rolling around in a wet pile of feces, covering its body from head to tail. *Why is it doing that?* Matt wondered.

Suddenly, it stopped moving and froze like a statue. Turning his head slightly, Matt saw that the one-eyed Komodo dragon had entered the glade, and he knew he had to perform a disappearing act, pronto. He had just enough time to duck behind a moss-covered boulder.

The Komodo edged closer to the tree lizard and Matt saw how alike they were. And somehow the young one instinctively knew that rolling in poop kept it from being eaten by an adult in its own family. The big dragon's tongue flicked in and out, identified the sickening odor, then slowly backed away. *Way to go, baby K. You're safe for now,* Matt thought.

One-Eye shuffled out of the glade and Matt counted to fifty in his head. When he was certain the coast was clear, he reentered the jungle to make his way down to the shoreline, and hopefully, the sea. Knowing that he was trapped on an island inhabited by Komodo dragons had shaken Matt to his core, and he struggled to keep it together. *Don't lose it now,* he told himself as he maintained a brisk pace on the sloping, slippery footpath.

There was something panting in the trees to his right. Matt stopped and listened hard but didn't hear it again. When he felt it was safe, he picked up the pace, feeling the cool swish of the palm fronds slapping his arms. A couple of minutes later he heard another sound. This time it was Sam calling his name.

Matt opened his mouth to answer but stopped when the Komodo emerged from the jungle at the same time he did. Fearing that any loud noise or sudden movement from him might provoke an attack, Matt was frozen in place, wondering if the animal could hear his pounding heart. Tensely, he waited and listened as his brother's shouts grew closer.

Soon Sam came around the bend of the rocky beach and yelled out when he saw his brother. "Hey, didn't you hear me calling you? Let's go, Matt!"

Wordlessly, Matt pointed to the massive creature that was slowly moving toward them with clear intent and purpose.

Chapter 8

THE ATTACK (SAM)

Sam left the cockpit and went on deck around 3:00 a.m. The night sky was clear, with alabaster stars dotting the inky blackness. There was barely a breeze to lighten the air but hopefully they would have the wind they needed come morning. *The sooner we leave this place, the better*, Sam thought. The rudder and navigation instruments were still cactus, but it didn't matter. They were shoving off at daybreak. No ifs, ands, or buts.

Sam knew they had a difficult day of sailing ahead of them. As soon as Matt took over the watch, Sam unrolled his sleeping bag and stretched out on the deck. It seemed he had just dozed off when the warmth of the rising sun woke him. Sam stood and stretched, trying to work the kinks out of his stiff back.

"Matt, let's get going. We have a big day ahead of us!"

There was no response from the cockpit or belowdecks. Sam quickly explored the boat, but clearly Matt wasn't on board. He wasn't swimming around the vessel, either.

"MATTHEW!" yelled Sam several times.

He stared at the island, not wanting to believe it. His brother was over there—the very place they were trying to leave.

Sam jackknifed through the water and swam as fast as he could before collapsing on the beach. There was no sign of Matt, and Sam crashed through the jungle, calling his name. Why wasn't he answering him? Had he fallen off the cliff? He retraced his steps until he was at the place where they had seen the tracks yesterday.

Sure enough, there was his brother, but he wasn't alone. Crouched about five meters from Matt was a ferocious looking reptile. It looked like it belonged in prehistoric times, where everything was either predator or prey. Sam's heart beat wildly as he took in the massive body, clawed feet, but mostly, the open jaws dripping strings of crimson saliva.

He knew immediately that they were facing a Komodo dragon. This was the largest and most feared lizard in the world, and they were trespassing on its turf. Sam swallowed hard. He began closing the distance between himself and his brother, hoping that the reptile wasn't threatened or hungry and would leave them alone.

Sam moved slowly and cautiously, never breaking eye contact with the Komodo. The only things moving on this lizard were its darting tongue and long tail swishing back and forth on the sand. Maybe it wasn't interested and they....

Suddenly, in the blink of an eye, the dragon pounced! Sam raised his hands in self-defense but was easily overpowered by the sheer size and strength of the reptile as he was toppled to the sand. Sam squeezed his eyes shut to block out the attack and felt searing pain as the Komodo sank its razor-sharp teeth into his leg. After inflicting this nasty bite, the reptile backed away but stayed within striking distance. Sam kept one eye on it as he leaned over and placed both hands on his wound, trying to stanch the flow of blood.

Matt watched in stunned disbelief as the reptile's teeth ripped into his brother's flesh, and he felt a hot stream of urine trickle down his leg soaking his bathing trunks.

Matt knew he was next and desperately grabbed two large green coconuts. When the Komodo took a couple of steps toward him, he threw them as hard as he could, and one hit the reptile squarely on its single, bulging eye. The long tongue flicked in and out of its bloodied mouth, but instead of launching another attack on either of the brothers, it turned and headed back toward the boulders. The Komodo called off the assault for now, but unfortunately it was between them and their boat.

Chapter 9

IN HIDING

Matt pulled Sam to his feet and hooked his arm around his waist, trying to keep them both upright as Sam groaned and leaned heavily against him.

"Sam, can you hear me?" His brother nodded his head but didn't speak. "We're going to hide in the glade we saw yesterday just until the coast is clear. I promise we'll find a way back to the boat, but right now we need to get out of sight. Okay?"

Matt kept talking in a low voice as they made slow but steady progress uphill. Sam was covered in sweat, moaning softly. They finally made it to the pool, and Matt lowered him to the mossy ground. Looking at Sam's injury made him feel queasy, but Matt knew it had to be tended to as quickly as possible.

"Sam, I'm going to clean your wound now. It might help if you close your eyes and think of something else. Hey, remember that black marlin you caught off the reef last year? What did it weigh… around seventy-five kilograms? That was the best catch of the season…"

Matt's voice trailed off as he dipped Sam's shirt in the pool and wrung it out; swallowing hard, he looked at the oozing, bleeding cut on his thigh. *How could this have happened to Sam?* Matt wondered as he gingerly touched the shirt to his brother's leg.

He replayed the attack scene in his head. As soon as Sam began walking toward him, Matt crossed his fingers and started counting. When he got to seven, the Komodo lunged! *If only I had reached an even number, maybe we could have gotten away,* Matt thought. *Well, we didn't, and clearly, I'm in charge until Sam recovers.*

The jagged wound was deep and bleeding freely, so Matt washed around the edges first. Sam gritted his teeth but didn't utter a sound. He knew how important it was to get this injury as clean as possible. The saliva of a Komodo dragon is teeming with deadly bacteria, and that combined with their venom makes a lethal one-two punch.

"We have to find a better hiding place, Sam. The Komodo will track us from our scent if we stay out in the open."

Both brothers looked over at the cave. Its dark entrance was less than two meters wide, with a heavy slab of rock resting across the top. It was black as pitch inside, and surely home to all sorts of creepy crawlies, but there wasn't another option. They eased behind the sheet of water cascading in front of the cave, and Matt tried to keep Sam's leg as dry as possible.

"Can we hide somewhere else?" asked Sam. "Caves creep me out."

"I don't know of any other place but it's just until nightfall then we'll sneak back to the boat. I'll go in first, then you follow. Try to keep your leg from touching the ground," directed Matt.

Matt squatted as he entered the cave and noticed that it smelled musty and damp like their grandparents' house in Perth. Sam scooted in next and lay on his back, breathing heavily. Matt stood and raised his arm, trying to determine where the ceiling was.

"It's pretty roomy in here, but I don't think we should go back too far."

"Yeah, I think we're in far enough," Sam weakly agreed.

Sam dozed fitfully most of the day while Matt kept watch at the cave entrance. At one point, he stood under the waterfall to wash away the urine from his bathing trunks. *One less scent for the Komodo to track*, he thought.

Around midday, Matt was alarmed to see the Komodo enter their grassy clearing, its forked tongue darting in and out of its mouth. It was searching for its prey—his brother. Matt didn't move a muscle, hardly breathing until the coast was clear. After waiting a full five minutes, he gathered up an armful of leafy branches and dropped them in a pile of feces. Matt wasn't sure what animal had left the poop, but he figured it didn't matter and dragged the leaves through the mound several times. The little Komodo watched from his tree perch.

"What do you think, Baby K? I got the idea from you, and if this keeps the big guy away from us, I'll be your friend for life. You know, the only thing that stinks worse than us hasn't been invented yet." The lizard slowly blinked his eyes as if he agreed with everything Matt said.

Matt arranged the foliage around the cave entrance, leaving a small opening for a doorway. After washing his hands downstream from the waterfall pool, he went in to check on his brother. Sam was burning up with fever, his skin dry and hot to the touch.

Matt helped Sam sip water from a bowl-shaped leaf which he drank too quickly, almost choking on it. Matt checked his wound and was alarmed to see that the bleeding hadn't slowed down, even though he had been applying direct pressure to the injury.

After some thought, Matt decided to construct a tourniquet and went outside to gather what he needed. There were several sticks lying on the ground, and Matt chose one that was slim but looked sturdy enough for the job. He washed it thoroughly and ducked back into the cave. Matt knelt down beside Sam and gently roused him again.

"Sam, your leg is still bleeding a lot, so I'm going to apply a tourniquet."

"Do you even know how to do that, Matt?" Sam weakly protested. "You haven't had any first aid training."

"Not official training, no. But I read about how to do it in one of my *Survive This!* books and it seemed pretty straightforward. If you continue to bleed like this, you could go into shock."

Matt folded his tee shirt into a triangle then wrapped it around Sam's thigh about five centimeters above the injury. He tied it off with a neat square knot, placed the skinny stick on top of it, then tied a second knot securing it all together.

"Brace yourself, Sam. I'm going to twist the stick slowly and steadily until I see the blood flow begin to slow or stop."

Sam groaned and clenched his fists. Matt watched the wound carefully, and as soon as the bleeding stopped, he tied the ends of the shirt together keeping it in position.

"I'll have to watch the time and remove it within two hours. You did great, mate."

Matt kept a close eye on Sam's injury and was pleased to see that the makeshift tourniquet was working. After he slowly loosened and removed it, Matt breathed a huge sigh of relief and lay down on the ground next to his brother. He needed to rest a couple of hours before tackling the next problem.

Clearly Sam wasn't able to leave the cave, but they desperately needed food and medicine from the boat, and there was only one person who could make the trip.

Chapter 10

NIGHT NINJA

At first Sam tried to talk Matt out of going, saying it was too dangerous, but eventually he realized that they didn't have a choice, so they came up with a list of essential items. Sam estimated that the entire trip would take under an hour if nothing went wrong.

"Hey, Sam, I'm going to do a little surveillance before I head out to the boat. Be back in ten."

Matt climbed up a tall, sturdy tree and looked over at the beach. Their boat was bobbing gently in the water—just waiting for nighttime sailing. The waning moon was bright, casting a peaceful glow over the little isle.

But looks can be deceiving. Were Komodo dragons nocturnal? Did they hunt at night, like so many other dangerous predators? That's the million-dollar question. The wind ruffled Matt's hair as he waited in his tall perch. There they were! Three Komodo dragons headed toward shallow holes in the sand and backed their bodies in until just their heads were peeking out. Matt hurried back to the cave to share this observation with his brother.

"Hey, it looks like Komodos are *not* nocturnal, so now we know to plan our escape for nighttime. Sam?"

There was no response from Sam, and Matt was alarmed to see his brother's eyes were glassy and unfocused, his cheeks hot with fever. He had definitely taken a turn for the worse, and Matt decided that he would leave for the boat immediately.

Matt squatted by the waterhole and drank deeply, then swiped his face with dark smudges of dirt for camouflage. A couple of years ago, he had a fascination with ninja warriors of old Japan and had a collection of replica weapons and books that told of their exploits. Tonight, Matt needed to be swift and fearless, like a ninja, blending into the night, completing the mission like a warrior.

Quietly he crept through the jungle, watchful for an ambush at any time. Matt breathed in and out in a steady rhythm. When he reached the sand, he crouched behind a boulder and scanned the shoreline for several minutes. There was no movement anywhere, and Matt was certain the Komodos were fast asleep in their beach burrows.

Slipping into the water with barely a ripple, Matt swam as fast as he could, finally pulling himself onto the boat with a grunt and shook out his arms and legs. He didn't waste any time locating what they needed, loading all the supplies in his waterproof backpack.

Turning to leave, Matt saw a picture of their family pinned to the cork board in the galley. It was taken last year when they had sailed to Cape York Peninsula and Matt blinked back tears. It was up to him to get them off doom island and he was determined to do just that.

Before leaving the sloop, Matt checked the radio and navigation instruments several times, but everything was still dead. Stepping off the ladder, he jumped into the water, going under at first until he got used to the weight of the pack. The return swim took a little longer but soon he was on the beach then pushing his way through the trees.

Matt breathed a huge sigh of relief when he reached the glade but catching a whiff of their stinking doorway almost made him gag. *It's like living in a toilet*, he thought, *but worth it if it protects us from further attacks.*

Sam opened his eyes when he saw Matt and rolled over to his uninjured side. "So glad you're back safe and sound. Tell me everything that happened," he said, squeezing his hand.

Matt told him about hiking through the jungle, the Komodos' burrows, and his swim under a moonlit sky. Sam frowned when he learned that the power and navigation equipment was still cactus. He clicked on the flashlight and looked at the supplies that Matt was removing from the large backpack one by one, lining them up on the ground.

"Check it out, Sam. We now have food, medicine, mugs, small saucepan, the hand crank flashlight, first aid kit, blankets, a small tarp, change of clothes, paracord, a multitool, and the lighter. I had to pack it twice but finally managed to get everything in there."

"Did you think to get a weapon, Matt?"

"I did grab the knife that we had yesterday when we explored the island. I was running out of time, so I focused on getting the stuff that we had talked about."

It hurt Matt's feelings that Sam didn't seem to appreciate what he went through to get the things they so desperately needed. He turned away and started building a small fire so he could boil water for tea, crumbling a couple of fever reducing pills and antibiotics in Sam's mug so they would dissolve.

They needed to make an escape plan, but the surge of adrenaline Matt felt earlier was gone, leaving him completely knackered. Right now, all he wanted was to go to sleep and wake up back in his own bed at home.

Chapter 11

HOME AWAY FROM HOME

Matt could see faint flickers of the morning sun through the leaf doorway but didn't have the energy to get up. He ached all over and groaned softly as he stretched his sore back and legs. Battling an ocean gale, being attacked by a primordial creature, and camping in a cold cave made Matt feel like he had fallen out of a second story window.

He glanced over at his brother and saw to his alarm that Sam's eyes were open, fixed on the cave ceiling. Not blinking. *Oh no*, thought Matt. *Was he…? No, he couldn't be.*

Matt leaned over and grabbed Sam's arm, shaking it until he felt his brother respond to him. "Water please," croaked Sam through dry, cracked lips. "Why are you shaking me?"

Matt felt relief flooding through him as he propped Sam up and held the cup to his mouth. "Drink this, and I'll refill it from the pool. And you need to take your meds. Hey, why were you staring at the ceiling like that?"

Sam was quiet for a moment then cleared his throat. "You thought I fell off my perch, didn't you?" he said with a soft laugh. "I keep thinking about when the lizard attacked me and wondering if I could have done things differently so we wouldn't be here." Sam swallowed hard. "And worrying that we're not going to make it out."

Matt felt like the adult as he reassured his brother. "It's not your fault that you were attacked—if anything, I'm to blame because you had to follow me to the island yesterday."

Sam didn't want Matt to feel guilty. "No, I don't blame you, or even the Komodo because it was just following its instincts. And to be honest, if I had told you that I *had* seen an animal with the binoculars you would have thought twice before coming here by yourself. It's all going to work out, but right now, bro, I need help getting to the loo."

Matt helped him up to a standing position and walked him over to the entrance. He peered outside, and even though it looked safe, he didn't think it was worth the risk.

"Just go on that pile of leaves here, and I'll bury them when you're done."

While Sam took care of business, Matt went outside, and using his hands, began scooping out a shallow hole in the soft, loamy dirt beside the cave. He was done after about five minutes and gazed at the beautiful, tranquil setting.

The waterfall cascaded down over large slabs of rock and partially hid the entrance to the cave, which is why it was such a smart hiding place. Matt could feel the spitting mist settling on his hair and arms, and it felt cool and clean. The pool was fed by the waterfall, and the water was so clear you could see the tiny pebbles covering the bottom. Surrounding the pool were patches of moss and lichen, which felt like the softest carpet in the world under your bare feet but became slippery and hazardous near the water. Tall trees, lush with leaves and vines, stood like sentries all around the perimeter.

Matt spied a straight branch almost six feet long lying at the base of the nearby kapok tree, and he walked over to pick it up. *This would make a good spear or a walking stick for Sam*, he thought, turning it over in his hands. Matt was excited about making something that could actually help them and couldn't wait to show his brother.

A loud smacking sound made Matt look up and he saw a sand-colored monkey perched in a tree, his head cocked to one side as he gazed at him with bright inquisitive eyes. One hand was clutching something, but Matt couldn't make out what it was. *Probably a banana*, he thought, as he went inside the gloomy cave.

Matt gave Sam his medicine and cleaned his wound, glad to see that the bleeding had slowed down from yesterday but concerned that it was still oozing. Last year Matt had written a report on Komodo dragons and learned lots of interesting facts about them. For example, their venom contains toxins that prevent the blood from clotting, which can cause its victims to go into shock. And if that happened to Sam, it was *game over*.

Sam tried not to moan as Matt dabbed at the area around the gash. "I'm going to place another rolled up blanket under your leg to elevate it," Matt said. "Maybe this will stop the bleeding totally."

"Yeah, okay. On the count of three," Sam said through gritted teeth as his leg was placed higher on the blanket. He took several deep breaths as the pain came in waves.

"I really could use a cuppa and something to eat." Sam felt queasy but he choked down most of a granola bar, several biccys, and a cup of tea. He knew that food would build up his strength, and he needed all that he could get.

Matt gathered up the dirty leaves where Sam had relieved himself earlier and buried them in the shallow hole he had dug outside the cave. *We'll have to spend one more night here because Sam isn't strong enough to make it off the island today*, he thought, as he picked up small branches and leafy palm fronds and brought them back inside.

Matt straightened the circle of rocks around the fire and stacked the sticks and branches nearby. He had shaken insects off the fan-like palm leaves before placing them on the cave floor and arranging their blankets over them.

"How's that for room service, mate?" Matt helped his brother lay back down and carefully elevated his leg on another rolled up blanket. Sam gave him a thumbs up and closed his eyes.

Matt organized their supplies and lined them up against the cave wall, so they were out of the way but easily reachable if they needed something. He made sure Sam was comfortable before taking up his position near the cave opening. Pushing aside a few of the stinky ferns so that sunlight could enter, Matt patiently removed leaves, dirt, and small knobs from the stick. Rubbing his hand over the smooth, clean surface, he unsheathed the knife and began carving a sharp tip at one end. He worked slowly and carefully, making small even strokes, always cutting away from his body.

Tonight, when Matt made a fire, he would bake the sharp point to harden the wood and remove any moisture from it. If he was satisfied with the results, then he would make another spear tomorrow so both brothers would have one.

Carving the hard wood was tedious work, and the muscles in his hands and arms were growing tired, but Matt resisted speeding up the pace. *Slow and steady wins the race, and I get to keep all my fingers*, he thought as he whittled away. Counting to himself helped to keep the rhythm and he took pleasure in this solitary task.

Matt made lunch at midday and helped Sam stretch and take a bathroom break. When Sam wasn't napping, they would talk about past vacations, or player stats of their national football team, the Socceroos.

Matt kept his eyes on the spear he was carving but heard every snap and rustle out in the glade. It was like his senses had become hypersensitive to everything around him—sounds, smells, sight, and touch. He was learning what things were normal here, and which ones were cause for alarm.

Daylight was coming to an end, and Matt hastened to build a fire before their space was plunged into darkness. Fire was probably the most important tool they had because it gave them heat, light, and protection from whatever lurked around the island at night. Dinner was tins of beef stew and peaches, which tasted surprisingly good, and cleanup was easy since they licked their containers clean.

Matt cleaned Sam's wound, applying fresh bandages, then made sure he took his nightly dose of medicine. The skin around the wound seemed less hot and swollen, but the gash was still oozing reddish fluids. Hopefully, Sam would turn the corner tonight.

Matt stirred the fire, tossing sparks around, and blew on the embers to reignite them. Sam watched Matt hold the pointy end of his spear just above the low flames, turning it until the wood changed color. He kept spinning it until the entire point was baked. Heat hardens the wood, making it less likely to splinter if it hit something solid, like the armor of a Komodo dragon.

"What do ya think, Sam?" Matt held up the spear with its deadly sharp, blackened tip.

"Aces, bro. Where did you learn to do that?"

"Do you remember that book collection *Survive This!* that Granny Sawyer gave me two Christmases ago? I bet I've read each book at least twice, but I have to say it's more fun to do this stuff in real life. Anyway, that's how I knew how to carve a spear and make a handmade tourniquet. Those books tell about actual situations where people had to rely on their wits to survive in hostile environments, like the Arctic or the Andes Mountains. I read about how this guy whittled a stick for hunting and protection, and it saved his life a couple of times. It went into a lot of detail about how to do it, and I just remembered the steps."

Matt was satisfied with his handiwork and leaned the wooden javelin on the wall close enough so that he could grab it quickly during the night.

Matt listened to Sam's soft snores. He couldn't quiet his mind, and his thoughts went to those dog-eared survival books resting on his book-case. What made those people special? He guessed that some folks took to the challenge of survival right away, while others had to be brought to the brink of death before they adopted the mindset of either victor or victim. *What were Sam and I?* he wondered.

Matt eased back on his makeshift bed and looked over at their door-way. He gazed at the stars through a space in the branches and found comfort in their fixed positions. *These are the same stars that Sam and I were looking at four nights ago*, Matt thought. *Please watch over us now and guide us safely home. We need some star magic.*

Chapter 12

SURVIVAL OF THE SMARTEST

A strange sound awakened Matt. His eyes flew open as he caught the quick movement of something moving along the cave wall. The spear was just out of his reach, so he slowly got into a crouched position and grabbed the edge of the blanket. He figured he could toss it over whatever animal was in their cave and drag it out into the weak morning light. And then what would he do? Would he have to injure or kill it? Matt could feel his heart racing.

Glancing over at Sam, who was still asleep, Matt began creeping closer to the wall where he could see the outline of the small animal frozen near the entrance. It wasn't a reptile—he was sure of that—because he saw that it was covered in fur. He made a lunge for his spear and grabbed it as the intruder shot out the opening into the clearing.

Matt was right behind it and saw to his surprise that their nighttime visitor was the same monkey he had seen the day before. It was an odd color, almost cream, and had a long, skinny tail that was bent at the end. The monkey was holding a bulky package of crackers in one of his hands but still managed to quickly scamper up a nearby tree. When it was sitting securely in the fork of two branches, it chattered noisily at Matt, and tore open the bag of crackers with its pointy teeth.

Matt pointed his finger at the monkey and shouted, "I'll be ready for you if you try that again." The monkey turned away and finished his snack, totally unconcerned about the threat.

Sam was awake when Matt returned to the cave, and he wanted to know what had caused all the commotion. He laughed when Matt told him about the monkey that had crept in during the night and stolen crackers from their stash.

"A white monkey—like a ghost!?" Sam laughed. "He'll be back unless we can figure out how to keep him out, which will be impossible without a door. Hopefully, we won't have to deal with ghost monkey anymore. I'm feeling better this morning so after brekky we should sit down and plan our getaway."

Matt was relieved that Sam was back in charge. He lit a fire to heat water for tea and laid out fresh mangos and granola bars for their breakfast. They sipped their cuppas and decided they would escape tonight when the Komodos were sleeping in their burrows. Sam would spend today exercising his leg within the confines of the cave and resting as much as possible.

Matt told Sam he was going outside to rinse out the bloody shirt he had used as a tourniquet. "Be right back," he called. *It shouldn't take too long to dry a cotton shirt in this heat*, Matt thought, as he knelt at the pool. The hairs on the back of his neck stood up as his lizard brain blasted out a message: *Danger!*

Matt slowly raised his head and looked around, knowing the Komodo must be awfully close. He spied it partially hidden in some low bushes not too far away and watched as the long tongue darted in and out of its mouth, trying to catch a scent. Matt knew that these reptiles could run extremely fast for short distances, and he was within easy reach.

"Sam, stay inside," Matt shouted as he took off running as fast as he'd ever run in his life. He scrambled up the closest tree, oblivious to the cuts and scrapes the rough bark was inflicting on his hands and legs. As soon as the branches began to bend under his weight, Matt slowed his ascent.

The last thing he wanted was to fall on the lizard, which was now directly underneath him.

It began ramming the tree, trying to shake out its prey. Matt was too afraid to close his eyes, but it was terrifying to see the branches shaking under the violent assault. He clung to the trunk and tried to come up with a plan. The Komodo stopped hitting the tree and began pacing at the base of it, staring up at Matt with its crazy, puckered eye.

Matt broke off a medium-sized branch and tied the bloody shirt around it, securing it with a double knot. He leaned over and dangled the branch until it caught the Komodo's attention, then threw it as hard as he could into dense foliage near the edge of the glade. It must have disturbed an animal because Matt heard snuffling sounds.

The lizard heard it too and lumbered off in that direction. Matt knew that it didn't end well for the animal but was grateful that his own life was spared. He listened to the sickening sounds coming from the bushes, quietly slid down the tree, and hurried back to the cave.

"Matt, are you okay?" Sam was frantic as he helped his brother inside. Matt was shaking all over and sat down near the wall, pulling a blanket around him. He drank the cup of water Sam handed him with one long swallow. Neither spoke as they listened to the feeding frenzy, occasionally peeking outside to make sure it wasn't getting closer to them.

It took the Komodo dragon about twenty minutes to finish eating, at one point slamming itself against a tree, which seemed to force the food down its throat. Finally, it stopped by the pool for a long drink, lifting up its head so the water would run down its gullet, almost as if it couldn't swallow normally. They watched it slowly shuffle out of the glade.

"I don't think it'll come back," said Sam confidently. "It's eaten a huge meal and will probably sleep on the beach for the rest of the day. You take it easy now and maybe work on that second spear in the arvo, yeah?"

Matt curled up on his blanket and gave in to the physical and mental exhaustion he felt, sleeping until the sun had passed its zenith. He awoke, feeling thirsty and hungry, and asked Sam what he thought they should have for lunch. A faint snore was his response. Matt looked at the lines of pain and exhaustion etched on his brother's face that weren't there before this trip.

Sam spiked a fever that afternoon and didn't have enough energy to walk around the cave, so an ocean swim was out of the question. They decided to double the number of antibiotic pills Sam was taking, which hopefully would stop the raging infection. Matt counted the pills left in the bottle and figured there was enough for a couple more days.

Matt did make a second spear, cutting a deep notch in the wood that his knife could fit into, and wrapping a long, strong length of vine around it so that the blade was securely fastened at the end. It was a serious looking weapon, and Matt was satisfied with the result. He placed it on the wall beside the other spear.

Their mood was somber that night as they watched the soft flicker of the fire. Matt looked over at Sam and said, "Mum and Dad must know by now that something has happened. Do you think anyone is searching for us? Are we going to be found?" Matt wanted to add the word *alive* to the end of that last sentence but stopped himself.

"Yeah, I'm sure that Dad's alerted the authorities and it's only a matter of time before they retrace our course and locate us. Think positive thoughts, mate."

"You know, you're right, Sam. We totally outsmarted that lizard today! I feel like we're living in prehistoric times and we have the word 'snack' written across our butts, but we *are* at the top of the food chain when it comes to brain power. Charles Darwin had it all wrong. It should be survival of the smartest—not fittest."

Sam laughed as he shifted his weight on the ground. "I hear ya! Let's get some rest so we can handle whatever this island throws at us tomorrow."

But Matt couldn't sleep. He tossed and turned and tried counting backward from a hundred, but nothing worked. He became aware of a strange low rumbling coming from the interior of the cave, almost like a vibration. *What in the world could that be?*

He turned on the flashlight and pointed it toward the pitch blackness of the cave. Matt grabbed his spear and began following the yellow cone of his light, shining it on the walls and the uneven ground. The narrow passageway of the cave suddenly emptied into a much larger space, and his mouth dropped open as he realized what he was looking at.

Chapter 13

CAVE OF SECRETS

The first thing Matt noticed were several wooden casks lined up in front of a wall. Beside them was a length of rusty chain coiled up like a pit viper, and the lumpy outline of more things hidden by a large, yellowed cloth that had mildewed and disintegrated in spots.

He tried to get his bearings as he swept his weakening flashlight over the walls, and then aimed the beam upward. The ray of light disappeared before it reached the roof, so he had no way of knowing the height of the cavern, but figured it was at least twenty feet.

As Matt gazed upward, he saw long, bumpy icicles hanging from the ceiling, which made the space seem even creepier. The air felt cool and drafty, like there was another opening nearby and damp droplets settled on his hair and arms. Matt could feel a slight buzzing as he laid a hand on the uneven surface of the wall, but the vibrating sensation dissipated as soon as he stepped into the opening.

Matt turned in a full circle with his light pivoting with him. This was a large space, much bigger than his bedroom at home. And speaking of home, the cave apparently had played host to more than bats and whatever else lived in dark, dank spaces because he was looking at the evidence. *Who had lived here and what had happened to them?* Matt wondered. It was time to get back to their little corner of the cave and share this discovery with Sam.

He headed toward their campsite and realized that he could be blindfolded and still find it by following the pungent scents of woodsmoke and poo leaves. Crikey, it smelled awful.

The sound of Sam snoring made Matt feel tired, and he knew he wouldn't have any trouble falling asleep now. He burrowed under his blanket—the cave was chilly at night—and kept his knife spear close at hand in case something or someone disturbed them.

The morning sun was up before the brothers. Matt opened bleary eyes and gave his muscles a nice, long stretch. "Hey, how'd you sleep?" he asked Sam with a yawn.

"I slept all night without waking up, which is an amazing thing," Sam responded. "My leg doesn't feel like it's on fire either. I guess the medicine is stronger than Komodo dragon venom."

"Fair dinkum, bro." Matt was encouraged to hear that Sam felt better and decided to keep his nighttime discovery to himself a little while longer.

Matt eased out of the cave, trying to steer clear of the stinking palm fronds, and headed over to the pool. He spied their monkey friend leaping from one branch to another in a nearby tree.

"G'day, mate! You're like a frog in a sock, hopping around like that," Matt couldn't help but laugh as he watched him. "Guess you're not out of food yet, huh?"

He knelt at the pool to fill the water canteen when a disgusting odor wafted his way; he sniffed at himself hoping he wasn't the source of it. Matt noticed flies buzzing over a wet pile of gunk nearby and he walked over, scanning the tree line for possible danger. He broke off a branch to poke around in the nasty patty and saw bits of hair and bone mixed in with the vomit. Matt wasn't hungry for brekky anymore as he tossed the stick.

Matt told Sam all about the Komodo vomit and how it was full of stuff that the lizard couldn't digest. "It was a total dog's breakfast, mate.

Very nasty. I may go back out today and bury it, so we don't have to look at it or smell it."

They ate Vegemite on crackers, canned wieners, split the last ripe mango, and washed it down with a cup of hot tea. Their food supplies were getting seriously low, and they knew they had to ration what was left. After eating, Sam swallowed his medicine and watched as Matt cleaned and bandaged his leg.

"Leg's feeling much stronger, Matt. Let's plan on leaving tonight. What time did you see the Komodos enter their burrows?"

Matt looked at his brother and knew it was time to share his news of the island's previous inhabitants. "Umm. There's something you should know first. Last night, I couldn't sleep, so I took the flashlight and explored deeper in the cave. And I found stuff."

Sam froze. "You did *what*?? Have you lost your mind? What if you'd gotten hurt? I wouldn't even know where to look for you." Sam raked his fingers through his hair and glared at Matt.

"No need to get salty, Sam. I had my spear with me and I'm perfectly capable of taking care of myself." Matt defiantly placed his hands on his hips.

"I'm not being rude, Matt, I'm being honest. You had no business exploring on your own like that," Sam argued back. He was trying to be calm but was genuinely furious with his brother. "That was dangerous and stupid. You know it, and I know it."

"Well, if it weren't for me, we wouldn't have any food or medicine and your leg probably would have fallen off by now," shouted Matt.

"If you hadn't abandoned your watch duty on the boat, then sneaked onto this island, the attack would never have *happened*," Sam shot back. As soon as the words were out of his mouth, he wished he could take them back.

Matt couldn't believe his ears. His eyes burned with unshed tears and he knew he needed some space that didn't have Sam in it. Matt climbed a shady tree until he came to a comfortable fork in the branches, leaned his head against the rough bark, and closed his eyes.

There was a soft *plop* on the branch below him, and Matt peered through the leaves to see the creature they had nicknamed GoMon, short for ghost monkey, staring up at him with curious eyes. "What do you want? More biscuits?" The monkey's response was to swing onto Matt's branch and smack his lips together.

Matt scooted down so GoMon could sit beside him. His eyes were a deep, liquid brown and his fur was almost white; patches of light tan scattered here and there made him look like he'd taken a tumble in the dirt. He smelled a little musky, but it wasn't unpleasant, and Matt watched as GoMon groomed himself.

The monkey pulled several bugs out of his fur and ate them as Matt began to tell him about the discovery in the cave and the argument with his brother. It felt good to get everything off his chest, and when he was finished, Matt was beginning to understand why Sam had been so upset.

"Okay, your turn, GoMon. What should I do now? Go back and talk to Sam?"

The monkey stretched out his hand and turned it palm up. Matt placed his hand on top and they stayed that way for a couple of seconds. "Jungle handshake, huh?" laughed Matt.

"Well, thanks for listening. I need to put things right with Sam." Matt climbed out of the tree and turned to wave at his friend.

Sam was standing at the cave entrance and looked relieved when he saw his brother coming toward him. He stepped to the side as Matt came through the doorway.

"Glad you're back, Matt. We need to talk and clear the air." Sam cleared his throat. "I'm sorry for my reaction when you told me about last night. As your older brother, I feel responsible for you and would blame myself if anything happened to you on this island. But the truth is you've proven that you're smart and fearless because you've handled everything since the attack, and you've done it well. I hope you accept my apology, Matt."

"I wish I had a do-over because if I did, none of this would have happened. You wouldn't have been attacked, and we'd be at home right now."

Matt sniffed and brushed angrily at the tears running down his face. "I'm sorry that I left my watch early and swam here without your permission. It's my fault that your leg is so messed up, and that we're being hunted by that monster so he can finish the job."

Sam was relieved to hear Matt own up to his mistakes and accept some of the responsibility for their unfortunate turn of events, but he kept his thoughts to himself because the last thing they needed was another argument. They needed to focus their energy on getting off this island before the sand trickled to the bottom of the hourglass.

"Matt, I appreciate your apology, and I meant what I said too. It's time to come up with a plan and I think whatever is stashed back in that secret room may help us. It's time to go exploring," finished Sam as he stood up and grabbed a spear.

Chapter 14

BOUNTY FROM THE SEA

Matt took the lead holding the flashlight, since Sam needed both hands to steady himself with the walking stick. They walked slowly through the narrow passageway, with Matt shining the light on the damp walls and down at the ground.

"I need to power up the flashlight, so the light doesn't completely die," said Matt, and both brothers stopped while he quickly spun the handle. Hand crank flashlights turn muscle power into electrical energy, which charges a battery and gives off light. They are lifesavers in emergency situations because they don't have to be plugged into an electrical source.

When they finally stepped into the space that Matt discovered the night before, they were amazed not only by all the things stacked along the walls, but also because everything was illuminated by an unexpected light source overhead.

"What in the world?" said Matt as he clicked off their flashlight. They looked up and saw an opening maybe a meter (about three feet) in diameter that allowed bright sunlight to pour into the dim cave. "Does it look like a natural hole, or do you think the people who were here before us cut it out?"

Sam studied the aperture above them. "I think it's part of the vent system from the volcano, in which case it would have formed naturally. It's pretty neat to see that patch of blue sky from inside the cave, isn't it? Wow, Matt, look at the stalactites up there! Some of them are pretty long. Do you know how they're formed?"

"They're made when dirty water drips down from the ceiling, right?" Matt asked.

Sam laughed. "Kind of. Stalactites are formed when minerals like calcium are left behind when a drop of water falls from the ceiling and it slowly builds up to form that icicle shape. Some people call them dripstones."

"Cool, but I hope they stay connected to the cave roof. Here, Sam, sit down on this boulder and rest as we look through all this old stuff."

"Yeah, that's a good idea. I can't believe how much that walk tired me out. But the million-dollar question is who were these people and what happened to them?"

"Maybe pirates visited this island and hid these things in our cave. But where is the treasure chest filled with gold coins and jewels!? All I see are big barrels, a rusty chain, cloth that is falling apart, and stuff that is so rotten we don't even know what it is anymore," said Matt as he poked at the lumpy pile at his feet.

"We should look around for a treasure map or a giant X somewhere, right?" laughed Sam. "I'm sure this stuff isn't pirate treasure. Hey Matt, how heavy are those casks?"

Matt walked over and pushed against them, testing their weight. The wood was waterlogged from being in the ocean, then stored in the damp cave, but they seemed intact; the iron bands that encircled around them rusted but holding fast.

"They're heavy and I could hear liquid sloshing around as I pushed against it," Matt said. "Do you think it's water or something else, Sam?"

"Probably not water, and they look like they're still sealed tight. If we had a crowbar, we could pry the lids off, but one of the attachments on the multitool might work. Too bad we left that back in our camp. Check out that pile over there."

"Okay, let's see what's behind door number two," Matt said as he peered under the tattered cloth, which may have served as a sail back in the olden days, and saw lots of pieces of wood, rusty pins, and a padlock that was dented and twisted. Underneath the rubble, Matt removed a bundle that was tightly rolled in thick fabric.

"Hey, this pile of wooden sticks looks like it may have been a pirate's treasure chest before it fell apart. All we need now are the gold and jewels," joked Matt.

He carefully unfurled the cloth and removed a pouch tied with a rawhide cord, a leather journal, and an antique writing instrument, which he handed to his brother.

This pen is obviously a valuable antique, thought Sam, as he carefully wiped it on his shirt. The barrel was made from a hard material and had thin strips of burled wood encircling the top and bottom, which were beautifully crafted. Sam carefully touched the split nib of the pen but didn't see any ink on his finger. He didn't know how much ink these old pens held, but it was either used up, or had degraded over the many years it had spent in the damp cave. Obviously, it had worked at one time, because there were handwritten entries on several pages of the journal which he was anxious to read.

While Sam carefully turned the fragile pages of the journal, Matt unknotted the cord around the pouch and dumped out seven unusual looking coins that were stamped with some type of mythical creature. They looked incredibly ancient, with bumpy, uneven edges, and were coated with a layer of tarnish. Several had small holes where the metal had worn thin. Matt rubbed his fingers over one and held it up to the sunlight to try and determine what the design was.

"Look at these coins, Sam. How old do you think they are?" Matt threaded one with the leather cord, then tied it around his neck, tucking the necklace out of sight under his shirt. The disc felt cool and heavy against his skin.

Sam was engrossed with what was written in the journal, and he looked up with irritation when Matt dangled one in front of his face.

"Knock it off, Matt. We need to get back to our camp and read this diary from beginning to end. The answers are in the journal."

Chapter 15

THE CAPTAIN'S JOURNAL

When Matt and Sam got back to their camp, the first thing they did was rekindle the fire so they could warm themselves up and boil water for tea. "Do you think it would be safe to sit in the sun for a few minutes, Sam?" whined Matt as he shivered under his blanket. "I can't seem to get warm."

"No, it's not safe. We're so close to getting away from here and I don't want to jeopardize it by risking another attack by One-Eye."

Sam sat close to the cave entrance in a patch of natural sunlight, and carefully opened the fragile journal. He sipped his hot tea as he scanned the pages.

"There are only half a dozen entries in this book but they're going to be hard to read because the handwriting is different than anything I've ever seen. There are ink blobs and fading on every page. Look at this letter, Matt. Is it an upper-case T or F? I mean, the words are beautiful with all the fancy, flowing script but it makes me appreciate something typed on a keyboard, you know?"

After about ten minutes of intently studying the journal, Sam cleared his throat. "Okay, Matt, listen to the first entry. It's written by the captain of a vessel that was shipwrecked off this island, just like we were. Here goes."

I, Jeremiah Gladwell, Captain of the Flying Cloud II, *a fully outfitted merchant ship of the British Tea & Spice Company, am writing this on 4 January, 1878, following a sudden and disastrous storm that took my ship and the lives of 27 crew two days ago. My navigational officer and bosun reported seeing a red sky at dawn on that day but the sea and wind conditions stayed normal until after midnight. When the storm hit it was with such intensity that we quickly lost two of our three masts to lightning strikes and wind gusts. Cloud suffered major damage to the hull which flooded the lower decks. Then it was just a matter of minutes before the entire ship was swamped and started to heel on the starboard side. Men were jumping into the sea, trying to stay clear of the ship going under and grabbing what they could to stay afloat. Myself and four other crew members: my 1st mate, purser, ship surgeon, and a seaman were fortunate enough to catch a current that floated us (and the brandy casks) to the shores of this uncharted island. We slept on the beach that first night then were forced to seek asylum elsewhere for a greater danger awaited us here than in the sea. This ends the first entry.*

"Don't stop reading, Sam! What happened to the captain and crew here on the island? What was the greater danger on land? What does 'red sky' mean?"

"Pump the brakes, Matt. It's from an old mariner's rhyme that said seeing a red sky at morning told sailors to take warning, red sky at night, sailors delight. We know now that a reddish sky around sunrise means there is a lot of water vapor present in the atmosphere, which indicates stormy weather is on the way. And I know as much as you do about what happened to the *Flying Cloud* crew. Can you bring me something to eat and my meds while I work on this?"

"Our food supplies are running low. I'll throw something together but don't expect much. I dreamed about Mum's chicken parmigiana and pavlova last night. Woke up and had to wipe the drool off my face," Matt laughed as he rummaged around in their food.

Sam munched on his lunch—it was an unappetizing combination of pale, vinegary sausages dipped in cheese sauce—while he read Captain

Gladwell's notes. Matt, wrapped in his blanket like a caterpillar waiting for rebirth, dozed fitfully by the fire. He was awakened by Sam shaking him and asking if he wanted to hear more about the crew of *Flying Cloud II*.

5 January. *I awoke with the sun and removed my spyglass from the oilcloth canvas bag that I had hastily packed during the storm and which I had strapped around my person in the likelihood that I would survive the disaster. Besides this journal and several navigational tools, I also included the miniature portrait of my beloved wife, Annabelle. Holding the glass to my eye I scanned the water for survivors from my crew but only saw floating pieces of the ship, which will either wash ashore or sink to the bottom of the sea. Then my astonished eye saw a small figure stumbling out of water and falling hard onto the sand. I awakened my officers and we rushed to give him aid. To my surprise I saw that it was not one of my crew members but the Japanese man, Takamoto, who paid for passage from Java to Australia. We gave him water and the surgeon checked him for injuries but found none. We were resting on the beach when there was a sudden movement in the sand and a large reptile creature emerged and crept toward us. We had never seen a reptile as large as this although we had heard rumors of such animals on the islands of Indonesia. Without provocation, it rushed the man nearest him, Dr. Blythe, the ship's surgeon, and brutally attacked him. Another reptile joined the assault, and it grieves me to say that Blythe did not survive. We hastily retreated into the trees and headed uphill as quickly as we could with the seamen carrying the weakened Takamoto. The only safe place for us would be high ground. Thankfully, we spotted a small clearing with a cave partially obscured by a waterfall and we entered it with a prayer of gratitude.*

My officers and I decided that we would retreat as far back as possible and discovered a large room that had an opening in the roof. We left the Japanese man there to rest and explored another passageway, one leading to the outside near the top of the island. There were several hot springs scattered around spewing odorous gases and steam and we took great care to avoid them. I was gladdened to see that we had two separate entrances to the cave and saw that this second one had direct access—although it was a steep climb—to the beach below. I told my men to roll the French brandy barrels that we picked up in Calais to the cave when nightfall came because we can't risk the wood drying out in the hot sun, and they may prove to be helpful to us in some way. I sent three of my crew out to forage for fruit, berries, anything that could sustain our energy. End of entry.

Sam and Matt sat in silence for a couple of minutes. "It's a bit uncanny how our situation mirrors what happened to the crew of *Flying Cloud II*. A storm brought them here and they were attacked by a Komodo dragon just like we were. I feel totally shook by it all, don't you, Matt?"

"Yeah. It's like their past is being played out by us in the present. I wonder if our fate is tied to what happened to them a hundred and forty years ago. Read more, Sam."

7 January. *It has been two days since my last entry. The seaman, Griffiths, has been grievously ill since ingesting poisonous berries on the foraging trip. Takamoto stopped us from eating them when they returned to the cave, but apparently, the lad had already eaten a handful. We have been tending to his nausea and cramping and are hopeful he will recover. The barrels have been stored in the cave. Every day I go up to the high bluff and scan the horizon for ships passing and are hopeful that we will soon be rescued. End of entry.*

"Do you think the poisonous berries are still here, Sam? I wonder how Mr. Takamoto knew they were dangerous."

"Maybe Takamoto was some sort of healer and that's how he knew they shouldn't be eaten. I need to visit the loo, then I'll decipher the next entry—we only have three more to read and I'm crossing my fingers that it ended great for these guys."

They both took bathroom breaks and Matt helped Sam stretch his injured leg. There wasn't any weakness in the muscles, and the wound was beginning to heal.

"My leg is feeling strong and I'm ready for the midnight swim to our boat. Hopefully, the Captain and his crew made their escape too." Sam picked up the journal.

8 January. *Young Griffiths died in his sleep last night. His suffering is over and when we get back to England, I will personally visit his family to inform them. Everyone will miss him, and a somber mood has fallen over our small group. Two unusual events happened today. Takamoto asked permission to go for a walk and I agreed but only if the purser, Chalmers, accompanied him. This island gives off a hostile feeling and it is my duty as Captain to maintain my crew and passengers' safety. Takamoto returned and said he found something he thought I needed to see before the cave light faded and so we set off down the main passageway. We veered to the right and found ourselves in a second hallway that was narrow and stuffy but still lit by ambient light from small cracks in the ceiling. I was shocked to see manmade drawings on the wall. They were of concentric circles with the largest circle the size of a dinner plate and two smaller circles fitting inside. These designs were repeated down the length of the wall. Drawn with something organic to the island, perhaps berry juice or charcoal from a fire? We also saw straight lines connecting these geometric designs. What could they possibly mean? Instead of returning to our chamber we kept going in the opposite direction which eventually led us to a another opening to the outside. This cave is riddled with a labyrinth of passages and rooms. When we stepped out of the cave, we found ourselves perilously close to sputtering, sulfuric pools. Near the pools we saw lots of rocks arranged in the same perfect circles as the cave drawings. The rocks were small and could fit in the palm of my hand and they looked more like ones you would find near a river than a tropical island. I became aware of a vibration or buzzing emanating from them and I looked at Takamoto to see if he could sense it too. His normally impassive face showed a look of concern and we quickly went back inside. As we entered the dim passageway Takamoto became faint, stumbled, and grabbed the wall for support. I didn't expect the stone wall to move but that is exactly what it did. Several large stones fell out and Takamoto and I were looking at a niche that had been carved out of the rock face. We pushed aside the rubble and pulled out a small wooden chest. It had a rounded lid and was secured with an iron padlock. After Takamoto regained his balance, we lifted it up and carried it* *back to our cavern. Chalmers and 1st Lieutenant Markham and I discussed how to best remove the lock. The light is fading so I will end this entry.*

"So, the pile of wood and twisted padlock that we found was from the chest hidden in the rock wall? I was half joking when I said it was pirate treasure but maybe that's exactly what it was." Matt looked at his brother. "We have to find out what happened to these guys."

Sam looked at the journal. "There is one complete entry then only a partial one." The brothers exchanged a worried look. Sam carefully turned to the section where they had stopped and read Captain Gladwell's words for the last time.

Chapter 16

INTO THE SEA MIST

January 9. *We were able to remove the padlock from the wooden chest but had to wait until morning light to fully examine the contents. There was an assortment of loose gemstones carefully tied up in a square of cloth, some polished and some uncut, sparkling and flashing in the overhead beam of light spilling down. Rubies, blue sapphires, emeralds, and purple stones were most pleasing to the eye. Neatly stacked on the bottom were three bars of gold. They looked like flattened bricks and had uneven texture and edges. We also found items that would be useful to any ship's captain and crew who were at sea for long periods of time: needles and thread, glass vials of medicine, candles, tanned animal skins, and sheaves of nautical maps which were soggy and faded.*

When I removed the last item from the wooden chest, a leather pouch containing silver coins stamped with a dragon design, Takamoto had a most unusual reaction to them. He picked one up, looked carefully at it, then threw it on the ground. He seemed agitated as he spoke rapidly in Japanese, then realized that no one could understand him. Speaking in halting English, he said the coins had brought us bad luck. Taking a stick, he traced a picture of the concentric circles in the dirt, then a picture of a reptile head with large, sharp teeth. I knew he was referring to the lizard that had attacked and killed Dr. Blythe. My crew had spotted the reptiles several times when they ventured out to get water and food and there had been a couple of close calls with them. And the mythical dragon on the coins did resemble the reptiles that inhabit this island. Takamoto kept repeating this word "tat-soo" and pointing at the coins. I dropped them in the leather bag, knotted the drawstring tightly, and put them back in the chest under the maps. My fingertips felt a little numb where they had touched the coins. Everything we had removed was replaced and the chest pushed against the wall. I sat down with Lieutenant Markham and we discussed what to do with the bounty – more than likely obtained by illegal means – and we decided to divide it up between the remaining two ship officers, myself, and Mr. Takamoto. The main reason for our decision was that the crew would have been well compensated at the conclusion of our voyage which would have ended in Australia, but with the loss of my ship that was now impossible. The Flying Cloud II *had begun her voyage in London, England and followed the Great Circle route around Cape of Good Hope in Africa. We then entered the Indian Ocean, traveled north to many lucrative ports in Southeast Asia, and lastly turned eastward on our way to Melbourne, Australia, where we had planned to obtain a large shipment of wool. Along the way, we had procured gold, spices, jewels, cloth, and enormous quantities of tea which were now lying on the ocean floor. Mr. Takamoto seemed very touched by this gesture and withdrew a waterproof oilskin packet from his coat pocket which he carefully unrolled. I leaned forward to see a hand-ful of plant cuttings, their roots carefully wrapped in a moist rag. "The best Camellia Senensis—green tea—which I brought from Japan. Will join my cousin in Victoria, Australia, to start new tea company," Takamoto spoke slowly and distinctly. "Many thanks for this wealth you give me to help dream come true." He bowed deeply with these words. We divided up everything in the chest except for the tat-soo coins and maps. There was a strange energy surrounding the dragon coins and I was glad to leave them behind. And then there is that matter of the circles on the walls and stones arranged in those strange circles. I do not have an explanation for them either, but I feel that our time is running out on this isle. I fear it will soon turn against us. End of entry.

January 10. *It was early morning when Chalmers rushed into the cave with great news! He had been stationed at the high bluff since daybreak searching the ocean for any sign of a vessel and when he spotted the tall masts and billowing sails of a passing ship he began signaling with the reflective mirror. It had gotten cracked during our swim ashore but was still functional. There was a mist rising from the sea and although he was able to make out the outline of the ship, we don't know if our island was shrouded in mist, making it invisible to the passing ship. Chalmers and I raced up the path to the lookout and it was clear that the ship had apparently seen our distress signal because it was changing direction, turning toward us. We returned to the cave to tell the others and hurriedly gathered our belongings and prepared to leave this isle. Into the sea mist. I will continue this entry when we....*

Chapter 17

THE PLAN

Sam stopped reading and put down the journal. "That's it. There are no more entries from Captain Gladwell. What about that word 'tat-soo' that Mr. Takamoto kept repeating? I wonder what it means. This is going to drive me crazy, not knowing what happened to them."

"Maybe the Captain's pen ran out of ink. But why would he leave the journal behind? Yeah, I was on Team *Flying Cloud*, for sure." Matt suddenly sat up. "They must have gotten away because there was no trace of the gem-stones or gold bars in the cave."

"Yeah, that's true, we didn't see them. But isn't it possible that—"

Sam's sentence was cut short by the startling appearance of the baby Komodo that often hid in the trees around their glade. He stuck his head right through the stinking poop leaves that served as their doorway and stared at them wide-eyed!

"Gaaah, what the heck?!" Sam jumped up and looked around. "What are you waiting for, Matt? Use your spear on it!"

"Lower your voice. This little one isn't the problem – One-Eye may be lurking outside the cave and your shouting just draws it closer. Quiet now." Matt wrapped his hand around the knife spear.

Baby K was frozen in place. Matt took the stick and lightly nudged the little lizard backward through the opening of the cave. It took a small tumble then righted itself and took off running to the closest tree. Matt started to laugh but then he spied something that made his throat go dry.

"We have a problem. The Komodo is just on the other side of the pool, trying to pick up our scent. It knows we're here," Matt whispered.

Sam quietly edged over to the doorway and peered between the ferns at the fierce reptile, who had clearly not forgotten about them. With a grunt, One-Eye lowered its heavy body down to the mossy ground. The tail swished back and forth, and the single eye closed as the blazing sun warmed chilly reptilian blood.

Sam backed away from the opening and beckoned Matt to follow. They tiptoed down the passageway and stopped when they thought it was safe to talk. Even a whisper seemed to echo loudly off the walls.

Sam spoke in a low tone. "One-Eye's tracking my scent, so you'll have to return to camp and grab the things we need for tonight and tomorrow. Everything else stays behind. Then we'll head up to the cavern where we should be safe. Safer than here, anyway."

Matt agreed and quickly returned with the dozen or so items they needed for their getaway, joining his brother in their new camp. Sam nodded his head in approval as Matt dumped out the contents from his waterproof backpack: paracord, the hand-crank flashlight, water, food for tonight, medicine, two blankets, a lighter, the journal, and bag of dragon coins. He leaned the two spears against the wall within easy reach.

"Yay, mate. You did a good job of getting all the right stuff. But don't you remember how Captain Gladwell and Mr. Takamoto reacted to those dragon coins? They're bad juju and they need to stay here."

"Okay, okay," said Matt. "The last thing we need is more bad luck. Do you think we should leave tonight or early in the morning? I guess One-Eye showing up is forcing our hand to leave Club Dread, and that's fine with me. This has been the longest week of my short little life. So, night or light?"

"Well, if we go at night, the Komodos are asleep in their burrows so we wouldn't be looking over our shoulder for them, and that's a huge plus.

On the other hand, a nighttime swim means we'd be exposed to sharks – they *are* nocturnal – and maybe box jellyfish. And will it be high or low tide? That's a factor too because if the tide is out, we'll be exposed longer on the beach, but the swim will be easier."

Matt was deep in thought. What he and his brother had gone through in the past week could be the plot in one of his *Survive This!* books. Now that the time had come to write the ending for their own story, he realized that he and Sam only had one chance to get this right. They wouldn't get a do-over.

"I vote for leaving at the first light of dawn, you know, before actual sunrise," Matt spoke with confidence. "We'd still have a cover of darkness, but with enough natural light to see what's around us. We'll empty one of those brandy barrels, which you can use as a personal flotation device. I'll pull it with the paracord, and your only job will be to kick as hard as you can."

"If we roll that old barrel down that steep path to the beach we'll have to go slowly, so it doesn't bust apart. The swim from the rocky beach will be a little longer, but it does bypass the dragons in their burrows. Okay, yeah… I think this plan will work and I like the idea of heading out before sunrise. Still concerned about the sharks, though." Sam looked worried.

"Also, we can make flammable torches to create a barrier between us and everything on this island. The firelight shouldn't wake up the Komodos because they don't burrow on that beach, but it may deter them from coming in the water after us if they do show up." Matt suggested. "We can soak the cloth strips in brandy, wrap them around sturdy poles, and then stick them in the wet sand. Kind of like tiki torches."

Sam looked at his brother with something like wonder. "Where do you come up with this stuff, bro?! Tell me what you need me to do."

"Hang out here while I go back to camp for the multitool that I forgot; it must have been hidden under a blanket or something and I need it to cut the branches. Maybe you can check out the passageways that the Captain talked about, so we know which one to use tonight." Matt took off at a jog.

As he neared the place where they had spent the past four days, a horrible odor stopped him in his tracks. It smelled like dirty gym socks but where was it coming from? Matt was shocked to see that something had torn down the fern and palm leaves that had covered the cave opening; he stopped and crouched near the wall. *How could I have forgotten to bring the knife spear with me?* he thought to himself. *What is going on now?*

Obviously the Komodo had crashed their space and it may be here waiting to pounce on him, so Matt thought hard about his next move. He was tempted to turn around, but he knew that was the cowardly thing to do. Was their nemesis still in the glade? He needed to know for sure. Matt slowly crept to the cave entrance and peered around the waterfall. The coast was clear.

He almost stepped on several porcupine-looking fruits that were bashed open and scattered around like tropical stink bombs. The smell made his eyes water and he pulled up his shirt to cover his nose and mouth. He recognized them as durian fruit—tasty—but had such a horrible odor that they were banned in public places like subways, bus stations, and airports.

Matt didn't even know that there was durian fruit growing on the island. *Who or what put them here,* he wondered? Something landed with a *splat* near his feet, and he looked up to see GoMon in a nearby tree cradling them like stinky babies. He was chattering loudly and held a fruit up as if to say, "You're welcome." He looked incredibly pleased with himself.

"Wow, thanks jungle buddy. Your poop grenades ran off the Komodo! You saved the day, GoMon, so help yourself to whatever food is left in the cave. Sam and I are leaving soon but we'll never forget you. See ya, mate!"

Matt cut six branches from trees in the glade then impulsively carved his and Sam's initials on the kapok tree with the date before heading back to the cavern.

Sam was shocked when he heard that the Komodo had busted up their camp then laughed when Matt told him how GoMon had dropped durian stink bombs everywhere. "I hope they keep One-Eye away for the next twelve hours until we're safely aboard *Zephyr*. We're going to miss that little monkey. He saved our butts for sure."

Sam continued talking as he paced back and forth. "Alright, let's go over the plan and make sure we have everything in place. I walked down both hallways mentioned in Captain Gladwell's journal and I think we should use the one that has the circle drawings because it leads to an outside path that's more direct to the beach. It's a little steeper but shorter by almost ten minutes. We have to be careful to avoid the sulfur pools—or whatever they are—but that's doable if we know where to step."

"I totally agree. Help me roll the first barrel down the passageway and stand it up outside, then we'll come back for the other one," Matt said as he removed the multitool from his pocket.

The brothers rolled both barrels outside, emptied one completely and tied lengths of paracord around it. Sam tugged on the lines to make sure they wouldn't pull off during the swim to the boat. They poured half the brandy out of the second barrel and tore up strips of cloth from the old sail which they twisted and secured around the tops of the sticks.

"They look like huge cotton swabs that a giant might use to clean out his ears," laughed Matt. "Help them carry them down the path to the beach and we'll stack them on the sand away from the incoming tide. We don't want them washing out to sea."

"Then we'll dunk the swabs in the brandy and light them at the last minute. I think this is a really good diversion tactic, Matt." Sam looked at his younger brother with admiration.

Sam and Matt finished all their preparations and hiked back up to the cavern to eat and get some rest. Matt unwrapped his brother's bandage and examined his leg. The edges of the wound looked a little red, but at least it wasn't oozing.

"It looks fairly good considering all the walking we've been doing. Take the last two antibiotic pills and I'll find us something to eat," instructed Matt.

They used the last moments of daylight to take a bathroom break before retreating to the darkness of the chamber. "Remember to be careful of these hot springs when we leave in the morning," said Sam as he gestured to a large one that belched every couple of minutes. "This one looks like it could suck a couple of toes off your foot!"

Sam and Matt went back inside the cave to wait. Their biggest test since they got to the island was about to begin.

Chapter 18

NARROW ESCAPE

The alarm on Matt's watch beeped softly at 4:45 a.m. The brothers had dozed off and on through the night, but it was difficult to stay asleep knowing what lay ahead of them. Matt turned his alarm off but kept his eyes closed while he said a prayer asking for their safe deliverance from this island. The dragon coin hidden under his shirt suddenly felt warm, and he absently rubbed the skin it was touching. Matt opened his eyes to see Sam staring at him.

"You ready to do this?" Sam asked.

"Yes, I am. Victory handshake?" Matt and Sam slapped, clapped, and snapped their secret handshake that they hadn't done in a couple of years. It felt good.

Matt briefly turned on the flashlight to make sure they had everything they needed in his waterproof backpack. He put it on and pulled the straps tight around his shoulders and waist. As they walked down the passageway, Matt trailed his fingers along the wall, and felt a slight buzz as he touched the circle drawings. At one point he thought he heard a man's voice wishing them *Godspeed.*

They exited the cave and Matt clicked the flashlight on to light up the geothermal pools. They carefully stepped around them and descended the steep path to the beach.

"Pry that lid off the brandy barrel," Sam spoke in a hushed tone. He looked around for movement of any kind, but heavy clouds obscured the moon, and this lack of light buried everything in darkness. *Well, hopefully, we would hear them coming after us*, he thought.

Sam and Matt worked quickly, dunking the tiki torches in the brandy, and jamming them in the wet sand along the narrow stretch of beach. Matt patted his pocket to make sure the lighter was still there. The tide was starting to come in, but they had plenty of time to swim to the boat before the flaming torches would be toppled by the incoming waves.

"Hey, Sam, you feel that breeze picking up?" Matt asked as they rolled the empty barrel into position. "I was worried that the winds would be too calm. It's a good sign."

"Yeah, can't wait to unfurl those sails and have the wind blow us away from here! What time is it?"

"Almost 5:15 - Full sunrise twenty minutes from now." Matt took a deep breath. "If you're ready, let's light the torches and get this show on the road."

Sam held the branches steady as Matt clicked the lighter and touched it to the tip of each one. All six torches were burning brightly and giving off a sweet brandy aroma. *So far, so good*, thought Matt.

They rolled the empty barrel to the edge of the water and Matt bent down so he could pull the end of the paracord free and wrap it around his forearm. "I think I can do the freestyle stroke with just one arm. We'll know I can't if we're swimming around in a circle," he joked.

"Wonder how far we'll have to wade out until the water is deep enough to float the barrel. Boy, this saltwater stings!" said Sam through clenched teeth as he entered the ocean. They pushed against the surge of the waves and soon the water was up to their waists.

"Hop on, Sam! Keep your head down and kick as hard as you can. I'll make sure we're heading straight for the boat," instructed Matt. He kept *Zephyr* in his line of sight.

Matt thought they were moving too slowly, so he placed the knotted paracord in his mouth and clamped down hard with his teeth; now both arms were free to move. He could hear Sam's kicks hitting the surface of the water and tried to ignore the discomfort of the barrel banging into his feet.

Matt tried silently counting backward from a hundred but got bored with that and came up with a chant instead.

One, two, three, four; me and Sam will swim some more.

Two, four, six, eight; we are doing really great.

Matt found that repeating this rhythmic cadence like an Army march made his strokes even and strong. He was so into it that Sam had to call his name several times before he heard him.

"Sorry, Sam. Did ya call me?"

"I looked back at shore just now and I think I saw one."

"What?!" Matt looked back at Sam in disbelief. Then they both heard the splash as the Komodo entered the water. Matt looked at the boat and estimated that they were about six meters (eighteen feet) away, which seemed achievable under normal circumstances. But a Komodo that knew how to swim, and who was bent on revenge, changed all that.

How fast can it swim? How can we defend ourselves in the water? These questions ran through Matt's head. Sam was lying on top of their spears, which were loosely tied to the barrel, but it would be next to impossible to swim while holding one, so they were useless. Matt dropped his end of the paracord and turned around to face Sam.

"You're going to have to push away from the barrel, swim like you're on fire, then pull me aboard the boat. Go, Go, Go!"

Sam kicked away from the brandy cask and swam toward *Zephyr*. He could sense that his brother was right behind him, but he had no idea how close the Komodo was to them until he heard the reptile bang into the empty barrel. Sam's scent was all over it and that captured the Komodo's attention for almost a minute. Its tongue darted in and out as his front legs clawed the sides of it, but the barrel kept rolling away and soon the Komodo realized that Sam wasn't on it.

There was another presence in the water that no one was aware of yet. It had been tracking Sam and Matt for about ten minutes, and now there was another creature in the water that was making a lot of noise. It submerged deeper and looked up at them with the unblinking stare of a predator.

Sam put on a burst of speed and his outstretched hand bumped against the boat. He touched his forehead to the hull both in gratitude and exhaustion before grabbing the stainless-steel ladder and hauling himself onboard.

Matt was right behind his brother and his feet barely touched the bottom ladder rung before he felt Sam lifting him straight up and into the boat. Matt jumped up and threw his arms around Sam shouting, "We did it! We got away!" But their joy was short lived.

Sam and Matt could hear the Komodo's clawed feet scrambling up the ladder after them and they were shocked to see its head pop up over the edge. Then it hooked its paw over the gunwale and flung its head from side to side, blowing saltwater out of its nostrils. It could have been a scene from a horror film.

"Matt, back up!" screamed Sam. "I'm going to grab the speargun!"

"No, Dad said *never* fire it out of the water, Sam!" yelled Matt.

"Like we have a choice," Sam shouted back as he started to go below where it was stored, but hearing Matt scream his name brought him back up on deck in a split second.

They were staring at the astonishing sight of a great white shark breaching out of the water a couple of feet from their boat. The Komodo dragon swiveled its head and the last thing it saw were rows and rows of razor-sharp teeth in jaws that chomped down with a bite measuring over 3,000 pounds of force per square inch. The shark ripped the Komodo right off the ladder, held it suspended in the air, then disappeared into the ocean with a tremendous splash.

Matt and Sam ran over to the side and stared down at a growing circle of red on the dark blue water. Just like that, it was over. Matt rested his head on the railing, closed his eyes and listened to the gentle lapping of the water against *Zephyr*.

The brothers stared at the island that was bathed in the brilliant colors of the morning sunrise. Every day here had been a struggle to survive; to meet the basic needs of food, water, and shelter. They were pitted against an animal that was determined to take them down, but in the end, it became the ultimate battle of nature versus nature.

Sam and Matt turned their attention to getting *Zephyr* under sail. They were going home.

Chapter 19

UNDER SAIL

Sam turned the manual windlass which raised the anchor from the sandy bottom where it had rested for the past week. It came up easily then they turned their attention to hoisting the sails. "Matt, let out the reefing lines and I'll check the halyard. We don't want the boom swinging around either, so after I release the boom vang, we'll ease out some of the mainsheet."

"How much sheet do you want, Sam?" Matt called as he worked the lines.

"I'd say about thirty to sixty centimeters of sail would be good," Sam answered.

"Okay, Matt, ready to raise the main," shouted Sam as he pulled on the halyard and began hoisting the sail. As it neared the top of the mast, there was more resistance and he had to wrap the halyard around the winch to finish the task. He adjusted the tension on the mainsail and boom, and then watched as a stiff breeze unfurled the sail and sent *Zephyr* skimming over the waves.

"*Woo-hoo!*" yelled Matt as the wind ruffled his hair. "We're headed home!"

"Hey Matt, come 'ere," said Sam. "Look, the instruments are working! I'm getting our current GPS location coordinates, and then we're calling

Dad and Mum. *Zeph* will be okay on her own for a couple of minutes." Sam punched in the numbers on their satellite phone and waited for the connection to be made.

"Hallo, Dad! It's me and Matt," said Sam his voice breaking at the end. He cleared his throat a couple of times and tried again. "Yeah, we're fine and are headed home." Sam held up the phone so Matt could listen and speak.

"It's me, Dad! Is Mum there? Can I speak to her?" asked Matt excitedly. Dad explained that their mum had just stepped out to the grocery store but that he would call her as soon as they hung up. "Tell her we're okay. We've had the adventure of a lifetime, Dad. I'll let Sam fill you in."

Matt listened to Sam tell their dad what had happened to them in the past eight days and he could hear his father interrupting with questions and exclamations of disbelief. They talked for a few minutes then Sam put the phone back on its cradle.

"Dad is going to contact marine rescue and he and Uncle Paul are flying out with them so they can pilot *Zephyr* home," said Sam. "They should be here in a couple of hours. Mum is going to totally wig out when she hears our story, isn't she?!"

"No doubt," laughed Matt as he rummaged in his backpack for his sunglasses. Suddenly he felt an immediate, searing pain on his arm and his first thought was that the multitool knife hadn't been secured and had jabbed him. Matt held up his arm and blood streamed from the gash onto the deck. His scream brought his brother to his side.

Sam picked up the backpack and shook everything out. Their mouths fell open in disbelief as the tree-hugging baby Komodo tumbled onto the deck. It lay perfectly still, its hooded eyes tightly closed as if it didn't want to see what was going to happen next. Sam picked it up by its spotted tail, careful to hold it at arm's length, and flung it into the water.

Matt wondered why Baby K had stowed away in his bag—*was it trying to escape its life back on that island just like we had done? Was a young Komodo's bite as dangerous as an adult bite?* These thoughts were all running through Matt's head as he watched Sam clean his wound and wrap bandages around it. Blood immediately seeped through, staining the white gauze.

"Sorry, bro. I can't believe this happened to you. Lay still and I'll go grab some pillows." Sam came back with a couple of pillows and a blanket. He put one under Matt's head and elevated his arm with the other pillow. "I don't want to move you, so are you comfortable lying there on the deck?" asked a concerned Sam.

Matt nodded. "Yeah, I'll be alright." He was trying to stay awake, but the rhythmic rocking of the boat and the warm sun quickly took him to slumberland. Matt woke up to the deafening roar of the rescue helicopter hovering above them. He tried to sit up when he saw his dad dropping onto the deck from the metal ladder hanging from the 'copter.

Matt's dad enveloped him in a big hug. "I'm here, Matt. We're going to get you and Sam home." Dad paused to wipe his eyes on the hem of his shirt. "These guys are going to treat your arm and transport you in that cool chopper, and Mum will be at the hospital when you get there. Uncle Paul and I are sailing *Zephyr* back and we'll all be together tomorrow." He stepped out of the way as the medics tended to Matt's injury and secured him in the harness.

Slowly, Matt was hoisted into the air, and felt immense relief when he was pulled into the chopper and unstrapped from the safety device. The medics repeated the rescue maneuver with Sam and soon they were lying side by side in the back.

It was noisy in the helicopter, but Matt liked the sound the rotors made as they spun through the air. *Thwap, Thwap, Thwap.* He closed his eyes and relaxed his tense muscles.

Chapter 20

HOME SWEET HOME

Matt and Sam were flown directly to a hospital in Darwin, where they spent almost a week recovering from their injuries and physical exhaustion. The second night there, Sam and Matt told their parents all about their adventure, starting with the freak storm and ending with the helicopter rescue. When Sam described his Komodo attack, Mum's eyes filled with tears and her hand covered her mouth. Neither Dad nor Mum wanted to let Sam and Matt out of their sight, so they took turns sleeping in a recliner in the boys' hospital room.

By the end of the third day, Matt felt like climbing the walls and begged his parents to take him home. "Can't I lay around in my own bed and get better?" Matt whined. "I miss Luke, Pickles, and all my friends. Please, please talk to the doctors, Mum."

"Matt, the doctors will release you when they feel that you and Sam are strong enough to go home. When you got here, both of you were dehydrated, weak from hunger, and had serious infections caused by the Komodo bites. Now you're doing great, and it's thanks to the wonderful care you're receiving here. So, no more complaining," said Mum with a smile as she smoothed back the hair off his forehead.

Sam spoke up from the other bed in the room they were sharing. "Mum, do you think everything that happened to us was because I lost my

St. Christopher medal? And thanks for putting it on a stronger chain." He patted it through his hospital gown.

Mum winked at Sam. "I think St. Christopher was still looking out for you and Matt even though it was hundreds of miles away in my jewelry box, darling."

Matt reached up to touch the dragon coin necklace then remembered that he had taken it off in the helicopter and shoved it in a zippered side pocket in his backpack. He wondered if it had brought them protection too.

The next couple of days in the hospital passed quickly, and soon Matt and Sam were cleared by the doctors to go home. They had to continue antibiotics for ten more days and make an appointment to see Dr. Ling at his office. Mum had brought the doctors and nurses a huge basket of home-baked goodies as a thank you, and they all gathered to say goodbye to the Sawyer family.

Coming home was like opening the biggest present under the Christmas tree. Even boring things like weeding Mum's garden seemed special, and Matt vowed to never complain about it again. Luke took turns sleeping in the boys' bedrooms, and Mum cooked all their favorite foods. They had one week left until school started back, and they were looking forward to seeing their friends.

Dad and Uncle Paul had thoroughly cleaned their boat after returning home, so Matt and Sam were surprised when Dad said he needed their help with something at Shorty's Marina one afternoon. They walked over to the slip where *Zephyr* was bobbing in the water.

"What's going on, Dad? She looks all spiffy and clean," asked Sam.

"I noticed something interesting on the starboard side when I was hosing her off. Come on, I'll show you," said Dad as they walked down the dock toward their sailboat. It dipped gently to one side as they all boarded.

Dad leaned over the top railing and pointed at something. "As I said, when I was scrubbing the salt residue off the hull, I saw this unusual mark near the ladder. What do you boys think caused that?" Dad pointed to a deep, jagged scratch that was about 15 centimeters long. "Did you run into something?"

"Yeah, the claw of a Komodo dragon," Sam replied with a grin. "That's where it was hanging, trying to decide if it wanted in or not. It gouged the boat pretty good, didn't it? Do you want us to help you patch and paint, Dad?"

"Well, if we patch it, then it's gone forever. On the other hand, we could fill the gash in with some silver marine paint that we have in our storage locker here. It would be a reminder about an experience that you may want to forget, though. It's up to you guys," said Dad.

Sam and Matt decided they wanted to keep it and spent the next hour applying the silver paint to the mark with small brushes. After the paint dried in the hot sun, they buffed away the rough edges. And instead of the metallic zigzag looking out of place, it looked like it definitely belonged there and had a story to tell.

"*Zephyr* has her own fierce battle scar!" laughed Sam. "Awesome!"

"It may be awhile before we take her out again, with school starting next week, so let's make sure everything onboard is shipshape," Dad said. They left the marina a short time later.

A week into the new school term, Matt and Sam found themselves swamped with homework, extracurricular sports, and hanging out with friends. Matt's school newspaper had a welcome-back contest for the most unusual vacation and his account of their Komodo adventure won first place. He cut out his story, *Terror Island*, and taped it above his desk.

A local TV station had contacted Bob and Sarah Sawyer several times about doing an interview with their sons about their encounter with the Komodo dragons. Although they weren't crazy about putting Matt and Sam in the limelight, they thought it only fair to have a family discussion about it.

Matt spoke up first. "Yeah, I'd like to be on TV and tell our story to everyone. It has plenty of action and a happy ending. Plus, it may help me with the ladies. I'll be a famous local celebrity."

Everyone laughed, and Mum said she would contact the TV station and see when they wanted the boys to come in.

Sam and Matt did the segment a couple of weeks later on Saturday afternoon. The interviewer, Ms. Rose, was mesmerized by their story and had lots of questions for them. They enjoyed talking about their adventure now that it was over, and they were safely out of reach of anything hungry or dangerous.

Sam read a couple of entries from Captain Gladwell's journal and when it was Matt's turn to share something, he reached under his shirt and pulled out the dragon coin necklace. Ms. Rose leaned over to get a closer look at it.

"The dragon design on this coin is so unusual and detailed. And it does look like it's from an actual pirate treasure chest! Wow, what an amazing souvenir to have from your adventure," she said with a smile.

Ms. Rose sat back and looked into the camera. "Well, thank you, Sam and Matt, for coming in and telling our viewers all about your incredible, once-in-a-lifetime experience. We really enjoyed having you both."

When they got home, Sam questioned Matt about the dragon coin. "I thought we agreed to leave those coins behind in the cave, so I was really shocked to see it today. Have you been wearing it this whole time, Matt?"

"Yes, except I took it off in the helicopter and didn't put it back on until we got home. It's cool-looking and I don't believe it caused bad juju for the *Flying Cloud II* guys or us. Besides, me wearing the dragon coin necklace isn't any different than wearing a St. Christopher medal, so what's the big deal, Sam?"

"I don't know that there is a problem, but Mr. Takamoto had a negative reaction to them, and I guess I do too. It's hard to describe it but I wish we—no, *you*—had left it behind on the island. I'm going to do some research to see if I can find a connection between all these things: *Flying Cloud II*, the dragon coin, the island, and the Komodos. Maybe, in the meantime, don't wear it until we know more, okay?" Sam suggested. "I'm going to bed. Night."

Matt flopped backward on his bed and clasped his hands behind his head. He stared up at the ceiling and thought about what Sam had said. He wasn't convinced that wearing the dragon coin brought bad luck, but he was willing to take it off for a couple of days. Matt untied the cord and dropped the dragon coin in the drawer of his nightstand. Before he closed the drawer, he caught sight of the baby Komodo claw that he had found in the bottom of his backpack when he unpacked all his stuff. He had thought about throwing it away but decided to keep it as another memento from their adventure.

His last thoughts before he drifted off to sleep were about the survivors from *Flying Cloud II*. *Did they ever make it off the island or were they swallowed in the mist? Who was on the rescue ship that the Captain spotted early that morning?*

Chapter 21

THE **PAST**

The next morning, Sam knocked on Matt's bedroom door. "Hey, can I borrow that dragon necklace of yours? I want to research the coin online and need it for the visuals."

Matt pulled it out from his nightstand drawer and tossed it to him. "Here you go. Is there something I could do to help?"

"Research all the tea companies in Victoria and see if any of them were established in the 1880s. Maybe you'll get lucky and find a connection to Mr. Takamoto."

Sam barged in Matt's bedroom after lunch. "I discovered some interesting facts about your coin, Matt. I'm quite sure that it's one of the 'Silver Yen' that was minted in Japan from 1870 until 1914. Emperor Meiji was restored to power in 1868, and two years later, he ordered new coinage minted. They had switched from gold to silver and began using the yen system, so new coins were needed. It was also called the 'Dragon Yen' because of the coiled dragon design on one side. The reverse side of your coin has a sunburst which the later coins didn't have, which means it might be very collectible." Sam handed him the dragon coin.

Sam waited until Matt slipped the necklace over his head before telling him the rest. "And guess what the Japanese word for dragon is? *Tatsu*. Remember how Mr. Takamoto kept repeating that word to the Captain, who spelled it 'Tat-soo' in his journal? Now we know what Tatsu means, but that still doesn't explain why it upset him," Sam pondered.

"Unless Mr. Takamoto connected the Dragon Yen to the Komodo Dragons who were roaming the island, and had already killed one of their group," guessed Matt.

Sam looked thoughtful. "Yes, that could be. Maybe he didn't think that it was a coincidence that the dragon coins were hidden on that island. And remember how strongly he reacted to the cave wall circles and rock circles? Let's keep digging for answers."

It was late afternoon when Matt got lucky with his computer search. He found a webpage about a tea company in the southeastern part of the country that had been in business for over a hundred and thirty-five years, and proudly boasted that their current green teas could be traced back to Japan. He hurried downstairs to share his find with his brother and parents.

Mum called Tranquil Minds Tea Company in Victoria and talked to the owner, Maria Kiyoshi. She introduced herself, briefly summarized her sons' adventure, and asked if Mr. Takamoto was related to her. Maria excitedly confirmed that her company had been established in the 1880's by two Japanese cousins who had brought tea cuttings over from the old country. She went on to explain that the business was called Takamoto Tea

Purveyors for over a hundred years before it was changed to the current name. Mum offered to send copies of the journal entries that mentioned Mr. Takamoto and was delighted when Maria told her to expect a gift box filled with their first harvest teas.

"Wow, you know what this means!" exclaimed Sam. "If Mr. Takamoto found his cousin and they started a tea company here, then that means they all escaped the island!"

"Aces! I was so worried that something bad had happened to the guys from *Flying Cloud,* so this is great news," said Matt. "Let's keep digging."

"Can you find out what these unusual circle designs mean? Let me know if you come across something," Sam said as he handed Matt a sketch of the circles.

A couple of hours later, Matt shared with Sam and Mum what he had discovered about the cave wall designs.

"Ready to be amazed? The circles in circles are called *geospirals* and they represent positive energy in the Earth. Lots of geospirals happen naturally; the swirl of hurricanes, spirals in shells or plants, and even human fingerprints have those circular designs. And the straight lines that we saw in the cave also represent lots of good energy—they're called *ley lines*—and are found in certain places on Earth. They are thought to connect important old landmarks and sacred sites, but not everyone believes in them. For example, the ley line that runs through Uluru is called the Great Dragon Line. This dragon thing is becoming our theme song, isn't it?"

The Sawyer family had visited Uluru in the Outback a couple of years ago, and although they chose not to climb it, they spent the day exploring the ancient sandstone rock. They learned that it was over 600 million years old, is important to the aboriginal people of Australia, and is almost as tall as the Empire State Building in New York City. Matt took lots of photos of it as the sun was setting, when the brown rock turned a brilliant red color.

"So, Uluru is not only an amazing place but sacred as well. You know, I did feel the energy swirling around when we were there," Matt solemnly stated.

Sam and Mum looked at each other and smiled. "The only thing you felt swirling were the midges flying around your head because you forgot to bring insect repellant," said Sam laughing.

"Yeah, whatever. So Mum, did you find out what happened to our Captain Gladwell?" Matt asked.

"Yes, actually, I had a bit of luck tracking him down. Since the *Flying Cloud II* was registered in Great Britain, I used the National Maritime Museum Library. The curator was extremely interested in obtaining Gladwell's journal as an artifact for their collection, and I agreed to send it to him. They had records showing he was captain of both *Cloud II*, and a later ship, *Running Seas*, in 1879. So, apparently, he did return to Britain after being rescued from the island. Now, do you boys know about the history of the original *Flying Cloud*?"

"Not really, but I figured there must be a story there," responded Sam. "Tell us."

"The original *Flying Cloud* was a famous clipper ship that was built in Massachusetts and set the fastest record from New York to San Francisco in 1854. It made the journey, rounding the treacherous Cape Horn in South America, in eighty-nine days, a record that stood for one hundred and thirty-five years. It later ran aground in New Brunswick, Canada, in 1874, and was burned for its iron and copper fastenings."

"Wow, that's incredible. I bet *Flying Cloud II* was built using some of her fastenings, and that's why it bore the same name," Sam mused.

"Yes, probably, because *Cloud II* was built soon after in London," Mum said.

"Kind of crazy that both *Flying Clouds* had sad endings: one ran aground on a sandbar and the other one sank," said Sam. "They should probably retire that name."

"Agreed. Well, now we know that Gladwell's crew got off the island and had good lives," Matt said.

Mum nodded her head. "And we also learned that tatsu means dragon, Matt's Japanese yen coin has an interesting history, and Mr.

Takamoto made his dream come true. So, I think everything is wrapped up nice and tidy, don't you?"

Sam was quiet for a couple of minutes then spoke up. "It's nice and tidy except for the fact that we don't know how and why those Komodo dragons were there in the first place. That's what I keep asking myself. Why?

Chapter 22

THE DOLDRUMS

Every sailor knows about the doldrums even if they've never sailed through them. It's an area of the ocean near the equator where a lack of wind and water currents would cause sailing ships to stall, sometimes for weeks at a time. Science can explain it: because the sun shines directly on the equator, it causes the hot air to rise vertically, rather than blowing horizontally. For centuries, sailors have dreaded passing through this windless region because as their ships became motionless, food and water supplies were often quickly used up. Sailors became ill, both physically and mentally, and the morale of everyone on the ship was affected.

The doldrums can apply to people too if they become stuck in a state of boredom and don't have the energy or desire to change their lives. They find themselves waiting for the winds of change to blow them back on course.

In the months after returning home from their sailing trip, Matt was busy with school, sports, and his part-time job at the marina where he helped Shorty with boat maintenance. Matt was in charge of checking battery and generator levels, hosing off the decks, and surveying the bilge. The bilge is the lowest part of a boat and all kinds of things get trapped there—most of which is removed with a bilge pump. What sailors call "bilge water" is a mix of fresh and seawater, oil from machinery, and other fluids. Checking the bilge was Matt's least favorite thing to do but it was all part of being around boats and learning how to take care of them.

Matt hopped on his bike and pedaled the couple of miles to his house. He leaned it against the garage wall and went inside through the back door.

"Hey, Mum, are you making ham and pea soup for dinner?"

"Yes, I am. It'll be ready in thirty minutes. You must be hungry, lovey."

"Yep, worked up an appetite over at the marina. I could smell the soup a half a block away and got really excited!" Matt said with a grin.

Mum looked confused. "You smelled the soup from down the street, Matt? But how is that possible? Hmmm… I wonder if the ham is bad?" Mum lifted the soup pot lid and breathed in deeply. She brought a spoonful to her lips and thought it tasted fine. "You're playing a trick on me," laughed Mum as she turned around, but Matt was already bounding upstairs.

Matt had noticed that his sense of smell was going haywire. All of a sudden his nose could identify things that other people didn't seem to notice, like the sweet smell of sunshine on the clothes his mum hung outside to dry, or the aroma of backyard barbies several streets over. But the scent that elicited the strongest reaction from him was blood.

After what happened at school last Tuesday, Matt couldn't deny that this was a problem. He was getting his math textbook out of his locker when he suddenly picked up the scent of human blood. He looked up and down the hall but didn't see a puddle of it on the floor, no one had a nosebleed, or a cut covered by a band-aid. In fact, everyone was laughing and acting normally. Everyone except for him.

Matt had to resist his strong desire to track down the source of the warm, coppery-smelling fluid, and ducked into the boys' bathroom to splash cold water on his face. He breathed deeply and slowly. *If this doesn't stop in a week, I'll talk to Mum and Dad,* Matt vowed to himself.

Matt put off talking to his parents; instead, telling himself that all these weird things were just part of growing up, kind of like when his brother Sam's voice changed. His face would turn beet red when Matt would tease him and tell him he sounded like a corroboree frog in the Outback.

After waiting another week, Matt decided to share his concerns with his mum as he helped her weed vegetables in the garden. She listened thoughtfully as he talked about feeling down and tired, taking one of Matt's hands in hers as he confided in her. Mum brushed Matt's hair back from his forehead.

"It's perfectly normal to feel like you're out of sync with yourself after what you and Sam went through on the island. Just give yourself time to heal and readjust," Mum suggested.

"Well, there is something else that's been wigging me out," said Matt. "My sense of smell is not working right. I can smell things from far away, like when people are cooking things, and I've noticed that all the marina odors bother me. And a few times I got a whiff of blood at school and my body reacted to it in a weird way."

"*Blood*?! What are you talking about, Matt?" Mum looked panicked.

"Like this kid got a nosebleed in gym after climbing the ropes, and it was all over him and on the floor," Matt explained. "But here's the thing. I wasn't anywhere near the gym and I could smell it. It's like I'm super sensitive to it or something."

Mum looked at Matt with worried eyes. "I'm sure it's nothing to be concerned about, but I'll call Dr. Ling and make an appointment for you to get checked out. In the meantime, don't fret about this. You did the right thing coming to me."

Matt was glad that he had talked to his mum, and hopefully he'd feel even better after his doctor visit. But in the meantime, he couldn't shake the feeling that he was like a ship drifting aimlessly in the doldrums. Sitting and waiting. Sitting and waiting. Sitting and waiting.

Chapter 23

METAMORPHOSIS

Matt and his parents went to see Dr. Ling later in the week. Matt explained what had been going on since he returned from the island, and the doctor took notes as he listened. He ordered some blood tests and told the Sawyers they should have the results in a couple of days.

The next school break was right around the corner and Matt was busy studying for his final two exams. He had cut his days back at the marina to just a couple of afternoons a week and was surprised when Sam showed up there unexpectedly one day.

"Hey, mate! Can you take a break?" Sam called out. "I grabbed some cookies Mum had just pulled out of the oven when she wasn't looking!"

"Come aboard!" yelled Matt as Sam lightly jumped onto the deck on the sixty-five-foot *Seas the Day* sailing yacht. "I'm just finishing up here."

"Boy, she is a beauty!" said Sam as he looked around. "Let Shorty know that I'm available to crew for them anytime."

"Not me. I think I've had enough sailing adventures for a while," Matt said as he took a big bite out of an oatmeal raisin cookie.

Sam looked over at his brother. He had overheard his parents talking about Matt going to the doctor for tests. "You know, Matt, you can always talk to me. We are brothers, but I like to think we're mates too. I know I'm bossy sometimes, but I can also keep my mouth shut and my ears open."

Matt nodded his head. "Alright, it starts with the doldrums…" For the next thirty minutes Matt told Sam what he had been going through, including all his weird symptoms.

Sam didn't interrupt once. He listened and nodded as his brother talked.

"What do ya think? Do I have some kind of island voodoo going on?" Matt asked. "I feel like I might."

Sam took his time answering because he wanted to choose the right words. "I don't believe in voodoo, so no, I don't think you're under a curse. You're probably not feeling well because we weren't eating and drinking enough that week, or maybe a mosquito bite made you sick. But whatever it is, I bet Dr. Ling can fix you right up."

"Do you really think it's something like that, Sam?"

"Yeah, it's like Occam's Razor: the simpler explanation is usually the correct one. Sometimes people make things too complicated and they can't see what's right in front of them. But whatever is causing you to feel bad, I'm sure it won't last. And I'm here for you, okay? Just like you were there for me on Tatsu Island."

Matt laughed. "Tatsu Island. It finally has a name—I like that! Thanks for listening, Sam. I feel much better. Let me wrap things up here and we'll go home together."

Dr. Ling called the next day with the test results. Matt told his parents that he had talked to Sam so they should all hear the news together.

"Well, the blood work showed that Matt's white blood cell count was high, which usually indicates an infection of some kind. Dr. Ling wants to run a few more tests so he can pinpoint what's going on," said Dad. "So, Matt, we'll run by the lab tomorrow after school to get that done. And grab a chocolate milkshake afterward, alright?"

"I'm not crazy about getting stuck with needles again, but yeah, I'll do it," said Matt.

The following week passed without hearing from Dr. Ling, and Matt told himself that no news was good news. The last thing he wanted to do was sit around the house waiting for the phone to ring, so he was glad when Shorty asked Matt to help him out with an extra job.

Matt was hosing off the deck of *Dream Weaver* when he had an overwhelming desire to stretch out on the wooden planks and soak in the sun's rays. Lately, he was feeling cold all the time, and had pulled a thick hoodie over his shirt right before he left the house that morning. Nights were tough too, and last night Matt had added two more blankets on top of his quilt.

He turned his face to the sun and closed his eyes as he scratched the dry skin under his shirt. *Gosh, that feels good*, Matt thought as he lay motionless on the deck. *I probably look like Pickles when he lies on that rock near the heat lamp in the terrarium.*

Matt sat straight up, his heart pounding as the realization washed over him. He knew what was wrong with him, and it wasn't caused by a mosquito bite.

Matt tried to shake off the feeling of impending doom as he jumped on his bike and quickly pedaled home.

Chapter 24

WHEN DIFFERENT WORLDS COLLIDE

Matt's parents weren't home when he got there, and he was relieved to have the house to himself. He grabbed a snack and headed upstairs to his room where he flopped on the bed and tried to analyze the situation.

Matt turned his head slightly and stared at his bearded dragon. The lizard was just sitting there waiting for the heat lamp to turn on, or a delivery of food to tumble his way. What kind of life did it have? And was that a life that Matt was destined for? He wasn't sure he had all the answers, but he knew he didn't want to be another Pickles in the room.

But all the signs pointed to it: the dry, itchy skin; feeling chilly; the acute sense of smell, especially to blood; and the lack of energy and focus. And this morning when he woke up, Matt noticed that the toes on his right foot were tingling with a pins and needles sensation. He gave his foot a good rub before pulling on his socks and shoes, but now he was aware of it again.

Matt heard his parents enter the house and braced himself for the conversation he was about to have with them. He went downstairs and asked if they could talk. At first, they thought that Dr. Ling had called with the results, but Matt shook his head and motioned them to sit down on the sofa.

Matt blurted out the epiphany that he'd had earlier that day. He could tell by looking at his parents' faces that they didn't believe him, even when he began listing all the weird symptoms that were bothering him.

Dad and Mum were quiet. They exchanged a long look with each other, then Dad spoke.

"Look, Champ, you've been through a lot and we understand that. The whole family is here for you, but… there's no need to make up this farfetched story about you turning into a lizard. That isn't even a remote possibility, and I know that Dr. Ling—"

Dad stopped talking when Matt stood up and removed his shirt. The dry, bumpy skin on his chest and under his right arm was now covered with iridescent scales. The reptile skin looked tough and thick compared to the human skin that it hadn't overtaken yet. Mum gave a strangled cry, jumping to her feet and Dad looked pale and shocked. Sam chose that moment to walk into the room.

"What's going on?" he asked worriedly. Matt turned around to face him so Sam could see what the problem was. "Crikey, Matt. Is that your real skin or is this some kind of joke?"

"What kind of joke would this be, Sam? Me pretending to be a lizard for laughs?" Matt asked crossly. He pulled his shirt back on and sat down on the couch.

Sam sat down beside him. "Sorry, bro. It just took me by surprise, that's all. When did you first notice this?"

Matt sat down on the couch and put his head in his hands. "Today. I realized today when I was at Shorty's that I'm more lizard than boy."

Mum sat beside Matt and pulled him in close for a hug. "It's going to be alright, sweetheart," she promised him, then whispered something in Dad's ear and slipped away to the study. "I'll be right back," she called over her shoulder. "Everyone stays put."

Dad sat on the other side of Matt and placed his arm around his shoulders.

"I'm sorry this is happening and that we doubted you, Matt. We're going to get to the bottom of this problem and fix it. I give you my word."

"Where did Mum go?" Matt asked.

"She went to call Dr. Ling. I'm going to make some tea because I think everyone could use a cuppa," said Dad as he went into the kitchen.

Dad and Mum came back into the den at the same time. Dad sat the tea tray down on the table near the sofa and began passing around cups. "This is green tea from Mr. Takamoto's company that we haven't had a chance to sample yet," said Dad as he poured.

Mum took a sip of tea, and said it was delicious. She cleared her throat. "I just spoke with Dr. Ling about Matt's situation, and he's going to stop by in thirty minutes to take a look at him. I said that would be fine with everyone."

When Dr. Ling arrived, he asked Matt to describe the new symptoms as he took out his notebook and added the information. He seemed most intrigued with the scaly skin on his chest and told Dad and Mum that he needed to remove some of it for testing. It was a painless procedure and was over in a matter of minutes.

As Dr. Ling was getting ready to leave, Matt remembered that his foot had felt numb and tingly that morning and the doctor asked to see it. When Matt pulled the sock off and held up his foot, everyone gasped.

There was a sixth toe growing right beside the baby toe, with a tiny but well-formed claw poking out of the top of it.

"Bob, I'm going to faint," whispered Mum. He helped her over to the sofa and gently eased her down. "Put your head between your legs," Dad instructed.

Dr. Ling told Matt to sit down as well as he closely examined the extra digit. "Hmmm. Most unusual. I'm going to clip a sample of the nail and surrounding tissue. Hold still, this won't take long." Dr. Ling put the items in glass vials and addressed the family. "I have a connection at the university here in Darwin and will personally take these samples over to be analyzed. You will hear from me very soon, and do not hesitate to call if anything else arises."

The Sawyer family was in shock over these latest developments. Mum stayed home from work the following day and kept Matt company. The phone rang during dinner and Dad answered it, motioning to Mum for a notepad and pen, so he could write something down. The conversation was brief, and Dad looked grave as he hung up the phone.

"Well, that was Dr. Ling, as you probably guessed. The skin and nail samples came back positive for a species that is non-human." Dad held up the piece of paper with neat, block lettering: VARANUS KOMODOENSIS.

"Matt is harboring cells from the reptile Komodo dragon," Dad stated.

Chapter 25

EARTH MAGIC

Luke, the family's Australian Shepherd, was worried. Something had returned with the boys from their sailing trip, a disturbing scent that the dog picked up on immediately but that lingered even after Matt had been home for a while. He was unable to sleep near Matt now because he couldn't control the growls that started deep in his chest or stop the hackles from raising along his back. He wanted to lick all the bad stuff away, but he knew that it would take more than that to make Matt better. Plus, his tongue might fall off, and that wouldn't be good. Luke understood hundreds of human words, and he was relieved to hear that Mum and Dad would be bringing in experts of a different kind. Dr. Ling might be a good doctor, but he couldn't fix this.

It was great timing that Matt had completed his end-of-term exams a couple of days ago, and school was tracked out for the next two weeks. He couldn't imagine walking the halls looking and feeling the way he did.

Mum and Dad had spoken with Dr. Ling to ask what course of action he recommended and were disappointed to hear that he wasn't sure if Matt's condition could be cured.

"We'll go in a different direction than modern medicine, Bob. There's more than one way to skin a cat, as my Gran used to say. Would you be open to working with someone who believes in another type of healing?" Sarah asked her husband.

"Yes, of course," replied Bob. "But I think we have to move quickly. Are you thinking of contacting someone from your center?"

Sarah Sawyer worked at the Cultural Center for Appreciation of Australian Beginnings, but everyone shortened the name to CAB. Their mission was to help everyone understand the history of the original people of Australia – the aborigines. These people had settled Australia over 50,000 years ago and held many interesting beliefs about the creation of the world.

"Yes, I would like to talk to Miss Kirra, who is a traditional healer, and see what she thinks about Matt's transformation. She is available this afternoon."

"Alright, I think we need to give it a burl, especially since Dr. Ling doesn't have a treatment plan."

Mum met with Miss Kirra at the center and was so excited about their talk that she invited her back to the house the following day to meet her family.

Miss Kirra zoomed up their street on a motor scooter painted with a rainbow and parked it in the driveway. Matt was peeking around the curtain at the front window so he could get a good look at her before she saw him. When she removed her safety helmet, he could see that her long dark hair was braided into tiny rows, with small feathers and shells worked into the hair. Mum answered the doorbell and motioned Matt away from the window.

"G'day, Kirra, please come in!" Mum greeted her excitedly. She introduced her to the family and suggested they all enjoy a cuppa and snack on the screened-in porch.

Everyone got comfy, even Luke, who jumped up on the love seat and snuggled next to Miss Kirra. He licked her hand and wiggled his butt from side to side in a manner unique to his breed. "I'm shocked!" exclaimed

Mum. "Luke is always a little standoffish at first, and I've never seen him act so happy and trusting with a stranger."

Kirra laughed and scratched behind the Aussie's ears. "This little wiggle butt may be one of Matt's totem animals, but we'll talk about that later! Matt, did you know that the aboriginal people of Australia are one of the oldest cultures on Earth? We are tens of thousands of years old!"

"That's a lot of birthday parties," Matt smiled.

"Yes, it is," Miss Kirra agreed. "Matt, what do you know about Dreamtime?"

"Ummm. Is it like when we dream about stuff at night?" Matt guessed.

"Dreamtime or The Dreaming explains how the world was created, according to my people," explained Miss Kirra. "Are we comfortable and ready to listen?" Kirra sipped her tea and cleared her throat.

"Before Dreamtime, the world was empty and completely barren. But then my spirit ancestors created all that we see now: people, animals, plants, mountains, rivers, flowers, everything. The Spirits are with us still; we honor them with our music and art, and in doing that we remember all that they have given us. I like to call it earth magic because when you take the time to connect with the land, water, and air, it transforms us."

"So, Dreamtime was the beginning of time?" Matt asked.

"Yes, but we think of it as the beginning that never ends. Dreamtime is at the center of everything that the aborigines believe, and it shapes us to be better people every day. Does that make sense to you, Matt?" Kirra asked.

"It does. Can I ask you something, Miss Kirra? What is one of the most important places to your people?"

"Uluru, formally known as Ayers Rock, is one of the most sacred places to the aboriginal people. It was created in Dreamtime by the Spirits and is still inhabited by the Anangu tribe today. There are paintings inside on the cave walls which tell the stories of the Creation. And most importantly, Uluru is a final resting place for our ancestral beings, which makes it holy and sacred," said Miss Kirra.

"Is that why people can't climb it anymore?" Matt asked.

"Yes, the government recently closed the rock to climbers, which is a victory for the Anangu tribe which lives there," Miss Kirra said with a smile. "Have you heard of 'The Uluru Curse'? Lots of people would take small rocks or sand from Uluru every year, thinking that it would bring them good luck, but instead were plagued with misfortune until they returned what they had taken. The Uluru Park Office receives more than 300 packages every year containing the stolen rocks."

Miss Kirra sat back and sipped her green tea. "There may or may not be a curse, but it does disrespect the land to remove things that don't belong to you, don't you agree?"

Matt sat quietly, thinking about Miss Kirra's words. He had taken some things from Tatsu Island, but it wasn't sacred like Uluru. Or was it?

"I took a few souvenirs from the island that Sam and I were marooned on, and I'm wondering if that is why I'm having all these weird problems now," Matt said. "Do you think Tatsu is a special place like Uluru?"

"I think all places on Earth should be respected because they are gifts from our ancestors. And your mum told me that your island had cave drawings of geospirals and ley lines, which means there is a concentration of positive energy there. So, yes, I would say that Tatsu is a very unusual place. Maybe those Komodo dragons were attracted to that energy as well," Miss Kirra mused quietly. "What did you remove from the island, Matt?"

"I took an orchid bloom for my mum, an obsidian rock from the volcano, a Komodo claw, and my Dragon coin." Matt pulled the coin necklace over his head, handing it to her. Miss Kirra lightly ran her fingers over the rough design.

"Wait. Where'd you get the claw from?" Sam asked with a confused look on his face.

"When the baby Komodo hid in my backpack I guess he snagged his claw on something, and it came off. I saw it when I unpacked my bag and decided to keep it as a memento."

"I never got the flower bloom, Matt. Did you throw it away?" asked Mum. "That was the reason you snuck away to the island in the first place, wasn't it?"

"Yeah, it was wilted and stinky, so I threw it away during that week we were in the cave," Matt replied.

"Yep. That was the reason," said Sam in a low voice. "A stupid flower."

"What are you grumbling about, Sam?" Matt asked. "I thought we worked this out."

Dad interrupted the fight before it got going. "Sam, please excuse yourself. Grab some biccys and go upstairs or outside."

Miss Kirra sat very still, deep in thought while everyone's voices rose around her. She slowly ran her hand through Luke's soft fur.

"Matt, would you feel comfortable if I took a look at your extra toe and scales?" Miss Kirra asked in a low voice.

Matt lifted his shirt and was surprised to see that the lizard skin had spread even more. Miss Kirra peered closely at it then carefully touched the toe claw with her index finger.

"I think I know what we need to do. I had planned to treat you here, but I don't think that is going to work. We need to return for the redemption ceremony," Miss Kirra stated.

"I'm sorry, what?" croaked Mum. "Return to where?"

"The island, of course. It wants him back."

Chapter 26

BLOWING IN THE WIND

Matt tried to talk his parents out of this crazy idea, but Miss Kirra had convinced them this was the only way he would be free of the Tatsu Curse. His words, not hers.

He desperately wanted to shed his lizard skin and go back to normal, so he was willing to try anything… except going back to that place. He suggested having the redemption ceremony—whatever that was—*here*, but his parents were backing Miss Kirra on this one.

That island had changed him. He and Sam barely escaped with their lives, and now the plan was to show up again and tempt the Fates. Matt shook his head. He didn't have a good feeling about this, but apparently, he didn't get a vote. All this earth magic nonsense sounded as crazy as what was happening to his body, but no one was listening to the lizard boy in the room. They were leaving in the morning.

Miss Kirra had introduced Matt's parents to Liam Andrews, a helicopter pilot who would be flying them to Tatsu. Captain Andrews served with the Australian Air Force as an auxiliary pilot and also worked with different government agencies regarding animal populations and migratory behaviors. The Indonesian Ministry of the Environment had contracted Andrews to compile information about the Komodo dragons on the boys' secret island and report back to them. Matt and Sam would be meeting Captain Andrews tomorrow morning at the helipad.

This morning Kirra had stopped by with last minute instructions for them. She told Matt to pack the three things he had taken from the island - coin, rock, and claw – in his backpack in a zippered compartment so they wouldn't fall out. She also told him that he needed to bring a bathing suit, towel, and a lightweight jacket because it gets chilly at night, and she didn't know how late they would be there. The most important item Matt needed to pack was something handmade or personalized by him that he would present to the island spirits as a gift.

Matt looked around his room but didn't see anything that he wanted to give away. He began walking around the house, poking his head in cabinets, and looking on shelves for the perfect item. *Jeez*, he thought, *this is like a scavenger hunt for dummies. I have no idea what I'm looking for, and there are zero clues.*

Matt walked out to their screened-in porch and flopped down in the hammock. Eyes closed, he reached up and grabbed the rope they used to pull it back and forth, yanking on it a few times to get good momentum going. *This is so relaxing*, thought Matt. *I should sleep out here tonight.* He opened one eye and stared at the wind chimes above him that were gently moving in the breeze. The slender, copper rods tinkled against each other making the most harmonic and calming sounds. *It's like nature's music*, Matt smiled. He knew what he was bringing to the island tomorrow.

Chapter 27

HELLO, OLD FRIEND

The Sawyers woke up before sunrise and had a quick brekky of tea, oatmeal, and sliced fruit. As Matt was helping his mum clear the dishes, he told her that Uncle Paul had agreed to come by in the afternoon and pick up Pickles.

"Why are you giving Pickles back?" asked Mum as she filled the sink with sudsy water.

"I don't think it's right to keep an animal in a glass box or a cage unless they're injured or being transported somewhere. I talked to Uncle Paul about it, and he's going to release Pickles back into the wild. Sometimes I look over at him, and he just seems sad, Mum. And I'm sure he's bored."

Mum ruffled Matt's hair. "Okay, sweetie. I think that's the right thing to do, too."

Dad burst into the kitchen. "Let's go, kiddo. Sarah, leave those dishes until you get back. I'm sure Andrews is already at the helipad."

They went out to the truck and Matt climbed in, dropping his backpack at his feet. Luke jumped up and landed in the backseat on top of Sam. Everyone laughed as Mum said, "Looks like I'll have company for the ride back!"

As they pulled into the lot where the helicopter was waiting, Matt felt light-headed and nervously wiped his sweaty palms on his shorts. He watched their pilot walking around the Bell 429 completing the pre-flight safety check with an employee from the airfield, and after Captain Andrews signed the checklists, the man gave him a quick but smart salute.

Matt heard the low rumble of Miss Kirra's motor scooter and watched her pull into the space beside their truck. Luke raced over to her and she bent down to pet him after she removed her helmet and hung it on a handlebar. "Are we ready to go and make some earth magic?" Kirra asked as she and Luke joined the Sawyers.

Mum answered for all of them. "Yes, we are ready for Mother Earth to heal this family and make us whole again." She embraced Miss Kirra. "Thank you," she whispered.

Dad introduced Sam and Matt to Captain Andrews. "G'day, Sam and Matt! Welcome aboard, mates, and please call me Liam. You can both be my co-pilots today," said Captain Andrews as he motioned them toward the waiting chopper. "We need to get this bird airborne, so please say goodbye to your mum."

Sam and Matt hugged their mum. "See you tonight. Be safe, and know that I love you both," Mum said as she gave Matt an extra squeeze. "Matt, you have lots of people going with you this time, and everything will work out perfectly. I'm sure of it."

Captain Andrews slid open the door, and the brothers climbed in and moved toward the rear seats. Luke was barking like crazy, and all of a sudden, he pulled away from Mum and jumped in the helicopter.

Dad reached in and grabbed the dog, saying, "No, boy. You can't go this time." Luke wriggled out of his arms and got back in the chopper where he took up position near Matt. When Dad started to pull him out again, a low growl erupted from Luke's throat.

Miss Kirra walked over and extended a hand to the agitated Aussie shepherd who licked it then closed his eyes. "Matt, kindly get your towel out so Luke can lay on it. He is going with us to the island today."

Matt looked over at his parents who shrugged their shoulders. It was obvious that Miss Kirra was in charge of this trip, so Matt pulled his towel from his backpack and dropped it onto the floor beside Luke. He rolled his eyes and buckled himself into his seat. *Yeah, put my dog in danger too*, he thought, and tried to squelch the sour feeling in his stomach.

The pilot buckled in his seat and began his pre-light checklist, flipping switches on the computerized console: checking the fuel levels, radio frequency, and engine temperature and pressures. Dad and Kirra sat down, buckled their safety straps, and adjusted their headsets so everyone could communicate during the flight.

The Bell was powered up and ready to go, as Captain Andrews spoke into his headset to the air traffic controller: "Lights, Camera, Action to go." This was helicopter pilot lingo that meant everything had been checked out and the aircraft was ready for takeoff.

They rose quickly into the sky in a smooth, vertical motion, then veered off toward the sea. Matt gazed out the window and saw how the sunlight danced across the water, lighting up the water and the occasional sailboat. It distracted him from his itchy skin that was starting to bother him even though Mum had slathered lots of anti-itch cream on him this morning. He closed his eyes trying to forget how uncomfortable he was when he heard Miss Kirra's voice crackling through his headset.

"Matt, what gift are you bringing to our island today? Tell me about it."

"Last year my dad and I made a wind chime for Mum which she hung on the sun porch. We used copper rods, tied seashells underneath them, and made the clapper from a piece of driftwood we picked up on Mindil Beach. I wanted to add something for Tatsu Island, so last night, Dad and I hollowed out a space on the clapper and inserted an opal rock that I mined at Lightning Ridge," explained Matt.

Miss Kirra was smiling broadly. "Matt, I'm not surprised that you choose such a beautiful and spiritual gift. A wind chime uses all four elements of Earth: air, water, ground, and wind, and is said to maximize *chi*, or life's energy. And aboriginal legend says that in Dreamtime when the Great Spirit was brought to Earth, it came in form of a giant rainbow. Wherever the rainbow touched the ground, beautiful rocks were formed, and their light contained all the colors of the rainbow. That's how opals were created! These gemstones have lots of positive energy, so I'm glad that you added it to the wind chime. Perfect!" Miss Kirra clapped her hands.

Captain Liam spoke next. "Hey, everyone knows that Komodo dragons naturally exist on only five islands in Indonesia: Flores, Komodo, and several more neighboring islands, right? So, that's why my employer, Ministry of the Environment, is so interested in your Tatsu Island. They are curious about how many Komodos live there, and of course, how they got there. How many lizards did you guys see on that island?" he asked.

Sam spoke up. "I only saw One-Eye and the baby that used to hide in trees in our glade, but Matt saw three adults burrow into the sand on our first night there."

Matt nodded. "And One-Eye was the biggest one that I saw on the island, but a shark ate him when he was trying to get into our boat. The other two that burrowed in the sand were much smaller."

"So, two females that you can confirm but I'm sure there was another male besides One-Eye. When we get there, I'll hike around the island to get an accurate count. So, here's a fun fact about Komodo dragons that may blow your mind. Did you know that they originated in Australia?

Paleontologists have unearthed fossilized skeletons dating from 300,000 to four million years ago that they know belonged to the Komodo dragon species, and they recently dug up one in Queensland that they named *Megalania*. It died out about 50,000 years ago and is the direct ancestor for the present day Komodo dragons," finished Liam.

"But how did the Komodos get from Australia to those islands in Indonesia?" asked Matt in a puzzled tone of voice.

"There were land bridges that stretched from Australia to islands westward, which allowed animals, and later people, to 'island hop' and move around. These land bridges closed when sea levels rose with the end of the last ice age," replied the captain.

"Gosh, that's interesting. We never learned that in school," said Matt.

"So, when saber-tooth tigers and other scary mammals were roaming the earth during the last ice age, giant reptiles ruled Australia?" inquired Sam.

Liam laughed. "Yep, that's a good way to look at it. Crocs and Komodo dragons that were three and four times the size they are now were definitely the apex predators in the Land Down Under."

"So, you mates are going back for some kind of spiritual cleansing ceremony?" asked the pilot. His eyes glanced at the boys in the rearview mirror.

"Yeah, I guess it's fair to say we have unfinished business there," Sam stated.

Matt looked behind his seat to check on Luke. He was dozing lightly and seemed comfortable, lying partially on the towel. They didn't have a leash, but Matt knew there was a length of paracord in his backpack that he would fasten to Luke's collar once they landed on the island. He wondered why the dog had seemed so insistent on coming with them.

Captain Liam turned his attention to the GPS locator on his instrument console and checked the latitude and longitude coordinates of Tatsu again.

Bob looked back at his sons and gave them a thumbs up. "We'll be there in a couple of minutes. I have to admit, I'm anxious to see this place."

Matt and Sam looked out the windows and spotted the small island, gray smoke encircling the summit. Their pilot landed the chopper expertly on a narrow spit of beach and they waited inside until the rotors stopped spinning.

Matt dug out the paracord and tied it securely around Luke's collar, making a loop with the other end so he could wind it around his hand. There could be no chance of him running away and risking an attack from the deadly lizards that were probably waiting for them, curious about the loud creature that had just landed on their beach.

Miss Kirra stood up and gave directions to everyone. "Wear your backpacks and walk closely together in single file. Liam and Bob will be first and second, Matt in the middle with Luke, and Sam and I will bring up the rear. We are going straight up to the glade, at which point Liam will leave the group to canvas the beach areas for Komodo sightings. Any questions?"

Matt wanted to raise his hand and ask about bathroom buddies but resisted the urge. Miss Kirra sounded like a teacher on a field trip, but it was nice to have someone who was clearly in charge and not intimidated by this place.

The group exited the chopper and looked up and down the beach. There was no sign of the Komodos or their burrows as they jogged toward the trees and entered the dense tropical foliage. Matt kept Luke close by his side on the narrow trail and breathed a huge sigh of relief when they stepped into the open space of the waterfall glade.

"Beautiful oasis!" exclaimed Miss Kirra as she raised her arms to the sky and smiled.

"Yeah, this is the best part of the island," Sam agreed.

Luke was hunched over the clear pool, drinking like he'd just run a marathon. Matt squatted beside him with the makeshift leash resting lightly in his hand.

Dad stood in front of the cave with his hands on his hips. "Is this where you had to hide out for almost a week? Unbelievable."

Sam spoke. "We'll give you the grand tour once Luke is finished over there."

All at once, there was a loud commotion in a nearby tree that made them all look up. And there perched on a sturdy bough was a white monkey, chattering excitedly and bobbing his head up and down. He grabbed a vine and executed a perfect somersault to a lower branch.

"GoMon!" laughed Sam. "Remember us?"

Matt walked Luke over to the tree and looked up. "G'day, old mate. We're back," said Matt.

Chapter 28

REDEMPTION

Sam and Matt led the group behind the waterfall and into the cave. Miss Kirra hung back a little as she rummaged around in her backpack and removed a cylinder of rolled green leaves which she lighted. Waving it gently in the air, Miss Kirra and Luke walked around the glade, then joined the others in the cave.

"Hey, what are you burning?" asked Sam as the earthy scent drifted over.

Dad coughed into the crook of his elbow, then cleared his throat.

Miss Kirra explained. "This is a smudge stick that I made from white sage, eucalyptus, and mugwort. As it burns, it purifies the space and replaces any negative energy with positive vibrations." She held the smoldering stick in front of her and tapped the ash into an abalone shell. "Matt, show me the rest of the cave, please. I'm getting a good feeling so far."

The entire group moved down the dark passageway toward the cavern room which was illuminated by the natural skylight in the ceiling.

"Wow, this place is full of surprises, isn't it?" asked Dad as he looked around the space. "So, this is where you found all the artifacts from *Flying Cloud II*." He carefully rubbed the yellowed, tattered sailcloth between his fingers.

Miss Kirra walked beside the walls, dragging her hand lightly across the uneven, cool rock as the fragrant smoke from the smudge stick encircled her. She smiled and breathed in deeply. "The cave is welcoming us with open arms," she murmured. "Please walk us down the passageway with the sacred drawings."

Matt kept Luke close as he and Sam led the others down the narrow hallway that led outside to the bluff. Dad clicked on his flashlight, and he and Miss Kirra peered closely at the geospiral drawings and lines that flowed across the rock surface. Matt could feel a slight buzzing in the air and knew if he placed his hands on the walls, his fingers would vibrate and pulse with energy.

Sam stepped out of the upper cave opening and motioned Captain Liam to follow. They were standing on one of the highest points on the island, and Sam was pointing out the places where he and his brother had seen the Komodo dragons.

Stepping carefully around the hot geothermal pools of water that spewed bubbles and gas, Liam made his way down the steep path to the beach. He clutched his "lizard lasso" in his left hand, a metal rod that had an adjustable wire noose at the bottom and was designed to stop an attacking Komodo in its tracks.

Sam was joined outside by Kirra and his family. "Captain Liam left to go Komodo a-hunting, so what's the plan for us?" Sam asked the aboriginal healer.

"I need your help finding the perfect soaking pool for your brother. Take my thermometer and locate one that has a temperature of around 42° C or 108° F. When you find one that isn't too deep—maybe up to your knees—place small stones around its perimeter," Miss Kirra told Sam and Dad. "We will wait near the waterfall."

Matt grabbed his brother's arm. "So, now I'm getting roasted like a beef brisket. This day just gets better and better," Matt said in a frustrated tone. "And if this doesn't work, what's Plan B? I mean, Dad isn't questioning her wacky ideas. She says *jump* and he asks, *how high*?"

Sam laughed. "I got your back, mate. I do think this is going to work, but you need to get your head in the game, okay? Gotta go!" He joined Dad, who was poking a long stick into bubbling mud pools looking for the perfect one.

Matt, Miss Kirra, and Luke strode through the chilly cave and back into the sunny, welcoming glade. They all settled on the velvety moss near the waterfall where Luke sighed deeply, closed his eyes, and rested his head on crossed paws. Matt had to grin—nothing disturbed the Aussie's nap schedule.

Miss Kirra smiled at Matt. "I know you are feeling nervous and doubtful, but if you open your mind and heart, you can leave this island a different person. Isn't that why we're here?" She waited for his answer.

Matt nodded. "Yes, I do feel nervous, Miss Kirra. But this place makes me feel like I'm not in control. And then my thoughts start going really fast in my head until they get all jumbled up and I can't make sense of them."

Miss Kirra nodded as she listened. "I can help you with that, Matt. So, right now, we are going to set your intention for today, which means you state out loud why you're here and what you want to see happen. Then you are going to repeat those words over and over until they resonate in every cell in your body, especially the *Varanus komodoensis* ones. Ready to begin?"

Matt sat with his legs crossed and breathed slowly and softly. He accepted the clear quartz crystal that Miss Kirra placed in his hand, wrapping his fingers around it. It felt cool and heavy. Matt cleared his throat and closed his eyes. He decided to give this his best shot.

Miss Kirra's voice floated gently over him. "State what you desire, Matt. Focus your energy and tell the universe what you want."

"I will be healthy again, and free of Komodo in my body. I trust this healing journey. Heal my body. Heal my body. Heal my..." Matt's voice got softer and slower as he repeated his intention over and over. He felt relaxed and drowsy and wondered how much time had passed when he opened his eyes, feeling calm and energized at the same time.

Miss Kirra and Luke had wandered over to the orchid plant but hurried back when Matt stood and stretched. Luke licked his fingers, and Matt bent down to scratch him behind his ears. Miss Kirra asked Matt if he was ready for the next step, and he nodded in response.

"Alright, let's present your beautiful gift to the island."

They hung the wind chime on a low branch of the tree where GoMon liked to hang out and stood back to admire it. The copper rods tinkled a tune in the slight breeze and the opal stone flashed and sparkled. Matt felt good about this gift and hoped the monkey wouldn't try to take it apart or eat it.

Miss Kirra, Matt, and Luke rejoined Sam and Dad. "TA-DA, your very own hot mud bath awaits you, Matthew!" Dad motioned to a bubbling pool that was off the path and partly in the shade of a coconut tree. Sam and Dad had placed small rocks and ferns around the edge of it, and Matt had to admit, it looked inviting.

"So, what makes these pools so hot and stinky?" Matt asked.

"Well, they are geothermal pools, which means the water is heated underground at high temperatures—thanks to that volcano right over there—and contain lots of dissolved minerals. The high temperature melts the surrounding rocks and turns them into clay or mud, which creates bubbles and the rising steam. Lastly, the stinky smell comes from sulfurous volcanic gases that seep through nearby vents called fumeroles. They are actually quite therapeutic," Dad explained.

Matt bent down and dragged his finger through the muddy pool. "It's quite warm but not blistering hot. How long do I have to soak?" he asked without turning around.

"It depends on several things," replied Miss Kirra. "We have plenty of time, so let's focus on getting started. Why don't you change into your bathing suit and lay your towel near the pool?"

When Matt emerged from the cave wearing his bathing trunks, his father quickly turned around so his son couldn't see the shocked expression on his face. He was horrified at how aggressive the Komodo cells were behaving in its host—his son—with reptile scales covering most of Matt's body above the bathing trunks.

Once Matt was reclining comfortably in the water, with steam rising around him, Miss Kirra asked him to focus on his intention and the words he had spoken in the glade. While he was doing that, Kirra invited Sam to tell her about their island adventure.

"Well, it was the first time that Matt and I had sailed without our parents, but we both were excited about it. I was looking forward to just hanging out with my little bro and making some good memories. And when the storm hit, it was scary, but I kept a cool head, and we survived the gale with the boat intact. The storm had blown us near this island, and after Matt and I hiked it looking for water and food, I began to feel like I wasn't in control anymore. We saw these crazy tracks in the sand, and then I had spotted a creature that I couldn't identify but I knew it posed a deadly threat to us. I was the older brother and responsible for our safety, so when I got injured, I couldn't do my job." Sam paused and drank from his insulated water bottle.

Matt kept his eyes closed, but he was listening to every word his brother said.

Sam continued. "Matt kept me alive after that Komodo attacked me. He cleaned and bandaged my wound, applied a handmade tourniquet, and made a nighttime swim to the boat for medicine and supplies. Then he kept us both alive by making spears, warding off another Komodo attack, and discovering the *Flying Cloud* campsite. The only reason we escaped was because he came up with a brilliant plan and pulled it off. Matt was—and is—brave, smart, and wise beyond his years. I'm proud to be his brother."

Dad wiped away several tears and draped his arm around Sam. "I'm proud of both of my sons and can't wait to put all this behind us." He walked over to Matt and kissed him on the top of his head. "You can do this, Chief. Believe in yourself because we all do."

Sam and Dad took Luke and headed back to the waterfall. It was quiet after they left, but Sam's words echoed in Matt's head. He never knew that his older brother felt that way about him and their time on the island, and it was a total game changer.

As Matt soaked in nature's hot tub, he could feel the tension and stress leaving his body. He repeated the words of his healing intention as he wiggled his fingers and toes in the bubbling mud. Matt could tell that the morning was sliding into afternoon as the sunlight filtered through the trees at a lower angle. The light reflected off something floating right in front of him and he scooped it up in his cupped hand.

"Miss Kirra, come here quickly!" Matt said excitedly as he stood up.

Iridescent reptile scales littered the surface of the pool. They were everywhere but on Matt's skin. "They're gone!" shouted Matt as he ran his hands up and down his chest. He hoisted himself out of the pool and stuck his right foot up in the air. "My extra toe with the claw is gone, too. This is the best day of my life! Let's go show Dad and Sam."

Miss Kirra clapped her hands. "I'm so happy for you, Matt, but there is something we need to do here before we leave. I removed the volcanic rock, coin, and claw from your backpack so you can return them to their rightful places. How should we do that?"

After some thought, Matt decided to drop the obsidian rock into the geothermal pool he'd been sitting in. "Rock, you are returned to the heat and gases that flow from the volcano." Miss Kirra nodded her approval.

Matt scooped up a handful of dirt and went into the cave, stopping in front of the wall drawings. He placed the soil on the ground and using his finger, traced a geospiral pattern just like the ones adorning the wall. Matt placed the coin in the center of the design and said, "Powerful dragon, guard and protect this cave and whoever seeks shelter here."

Matt stood under the waterfall in the glade to rinse away any residue from the pool and gave a victory yell. Dad looked over and shaded his eyes with his hand.

"Did it work, son?" he asked as he and Sam trotted over. Luke was close on their heels as they surrounded him. "Would you look at that healthy pink glow!" Dad laughed as he ran his hand over Matt's smooth skin that was totally free of the bumpy scales.

They hugged and laughed as Matt turned around in a circle. "No dragon armor or extra toes. Feel like a new and improved me! I have one thing left to do, then we can blow this popsicle stand."

Matt went over to the tree where the baby Komodo liked to hide and buried the claw in a shallow hole at the base of it. "Rest in peace, little mate."

Captain Liam entered the glade and was delighted to see that Matt was once again in good health. "Congratulations, Matt! This is great news! Well, I have my Komodo count, so we can take off any time you guys are ready."

Dad asked, "How many did you locate, Liam?"

"This *bank* of Komodos—that's what a group of Komodos is called— had five in all: two males, two females, and a baby hiding out in a tree near the beach. This isn't the time of year when their eggs hatch, so the data is probably accurate. I will pass this information along to the Ministry of the Environment when we return. Alrighty, looks like everyone met their goals today so let's head out."

Dad and Captain Liam led the group down the trail but stopped abruptly when they reached the beach where the helicopter was waiting. Captain had raised a fist in the air which was a military signal for "stop."

Sam turned to Matt and whispered, "There are several Komodos on the sand checking out the chopper. Make sure Luke stays quiet."

Matt knelt on the ground beside the dog, and lightly cupped his muzzle as he whispered *shush* over and over. "It's okay, boy. Stay quiet." Dogs are able to sense our emotions and even read facial expressions, so Matt was trying to appear calm and unconcerned about the threat.

His mind was racing. *This is déjà vu times ten*, Matt thought. *Sam and I escaped from this island before, but what are the odds we could do it again?*

Chapter 29

GUWAYU

Dad picked up Luke and the group raced back up the narrow jungle path, reaching the waterfall clearing in record time. They felt safe there in the enclosed area, and collapsed on the damp, mossy carpet trying to catch their breath. The Aussie laid his head on Matt's lap and whimpered softly.

Captain Liam spoke first. "This is unbelievable, mates. All of the Komodos were on the opposite side of the island when I spotted them earlier this morning, but apparently they followed me back to our beach. I didn't realize they were tracking me." He cleared his throat nervously.

"I say we go on the offensive with these guys," Dad suggested. "We aren't going to wait until they decide to leave the beach, or worse, be attacked like my boys were. Show me how to use that lizard lasso, Liam." Dad watched closely as Liam demonstrated how it worked.

Matt joined Sam at the kapok tree that loomed over the northeastern side of the glade. He watched as his brother lightly traced his fingers over the initials and date he had carved in the trunk the day before their escape.

"Never thought we'd be back, but here we are starring in the same movie. *Tatsu Island: The Sequel.*" Sam shook his head. "What do you think we should do, Matt?"

"I think we should create a diversion on the beach. If we can lure the Komodos away from the chopper, Captain Liam can hop in and fire it up," Matt said.

"And the noise and wind from the rotors should keep them away," Sam nodded his head as he listened. "A simple plan, but simple is good. Let's go talk to Dad and the others."

Matt and Sam walked over to the group to share their idea. Dad and Captain Liam were talking about how to best handle the Komodo threat, while Miss Kirra sat a couple of feet away, stroking Luke's fur and looking unusually subdued.

"Hey, we have a suggestion," Sam said. "It's a straightforward plan without any frills, but Matt and I think it may work. Tell 'em, Matt."

"We'll create a distraction that lures the dragons down the beach away from the helicopter. As soon as he has a clear path, Captain Liam hauls butt to the chopper and starts up the engines. Once the rotors are spinning, creating a little sandstorm, the reptiles *should* stay where they are, at which point we all jump on board and wave goodbye."

"It's not going to be that simple, boys," Liam cautioned. "I have to release the tie-down straps on the blades and make sure the skids are free of any sand or debris before I get in the cockpit and start the take-off procedures. And I won't have anyone watching my back outside while I'm doing those things." Liam rubbed the back of the neck and sighed. "But I'm willing to give it a burl."

"Matt, what kind of distraction are you thinking of?" Dad inquired.

"The three of us would run onto the beach, making all kinds of noise, and hurl coconuts at them. If we can get one Komodo to turn around and retreat, the other two will probably follow. We'd have the element of surprise, and if we stay together, they might think we're too big and scary to attack. Sam and I will also have long sticks to jab at them if they get too close. What do ya think?" Matt looked from Liam to his dad.

"So, let me understand this," Dad said. "We surprise them near the helicopter and herd them toward the southern end of the beach. If we're lucky enough to make them move, what's going to prevent them from following us back to the helicopter?"

Sam answered, "We hold position until the rotors start spinning, and hopefully all the noise and swirling sand will confuse them, and they stay put. And then we walk backward maintaining eye contact, so we're ready if they charge us."

Miss Kirra spoke for the first time. "I think this plan will work, but everyone must agree not to harm any Komodos because this is their home, and we are the uninvited visitors. Luke and I will stay out of the way and visualize a positive outcome."

Dad asked for a group vote, and it was "aye" from everyone. Sam and Matt cut three long, sturdy branches, quickly stripped them of leaves and twigs, then unzipped their backpacks and shoved the sticks down as far as they would go. Dad took the remaining branch and they followed Liam's lead as he led them quickly down the path that cut through the jungle.

They reached the beach and almost tripped on the plentiful coconuts that lay scattered on the sand. Some were green, and a few were split in half, and Sam grabbed as many as he could hold and passed them back to his brother. When he looked behind Matt, he saw Miss Kirra carrying Luke and making her way carefully down the path, but she didn't meet his eyes. Her gaze was focused beyond him, seeing something only she could see.

The Komodos didn't know they were sharing the beach with anyone as they sunbathed near the helicopter. The largest one rested its head on a skid partially buried in the sand and the other two lizards were lying head to tail next to each other.

Dad stood between his sons as they looked over at the somnolent reptiles. "Let me go first, then follow closely behind. Ready, go!"

They ran onto the beach whooping at the top of their lungs. It was like a scene from the American Wild West, when bands of Native American hunters would swoop down upon herds of buffalo, hoping to secure enough meat and hides for the coming winter.

The Komodo dragons rose clumsily from the sand and were facing their attackers, tongues darting in and out as they tried to figure out what was happening. The large male that had been lounging underneath the chopper was hit in the snout by a hefty coconut, which it clearly didn't like. It turned around and began moving away from the group, its tail swishing back and forth as it picked up speed on the damp sand.

The two remaining Komodos weren't interested in sticking around either and they set off in the same direction. The Sawyers followed them at a safe distance, and Dad kept glancing back so he would know when Liam was ready for them.

Suddenly, there was a lot of commotion at the helicopter. "Dad, what's going on?" asked Sam as the sounds of yelling and frenzied barking reached them.

"Not sure," responded Dad. "But we're heading back! Let's move quickly and fingers crossed these guys don't follow us."

Miss Kirra and Luke were half hidden by thick foliage where the jungle ended and the beach started, but they still had a good sightline to the helicopter and the ocean beyond. They watched as the reptiles retreated down the shore.

Liam crouched down beside them and scratched Luke behind his ears. "They're far enough away now, so I'm going over to start takeoff preparations. You guys stay here, and I'll wave to you when you can board."

The pilot jogged toward the chopper feeling good about the whole plan. *This was almost too easy*, he thought to himself. Suddenly, there was a tremendous crash, and as he half turned, he saw a huge Komodo barreling his way. It was sprinting on its powerful little legs, its eyes locked on him like a heat-seeking missile.

Luke saw what was happening and jumped out of Miss Kirra's lap in hot pursuit. "Luke, come back!" she yelled to the Aussie shepherd. She snatched up a couple of coconuts and took off after him.

The dog quickly closed in on the Komodo and began snapping and nipping at its tail, which was enough to pull the reptile's attention away from Liam. The pilot bolted up the steps to the chopper and wrenched open the door, falling into the cockpit. Liam felt blindly behind his seat and with a sigh of relief wrapped his hand around what he was looking for, pulling it free of its harness.

The Komodo decided to put a stop to Luke's aggressive attack, and with a whiplike movement of its enormous tail, sent the dog flying into the air. Luke landed hard and wasn't able to move away as the reptile pinned him to the sand and flexed its jaws, dripping red-tinged saliva onto the dog's belly.

Kirra jumped on the Komodo's back and leaned over to shove a coconut between the open jaws, pushing it in as far as it would go. She rolled off the gagging Komodo as it thrashed around, trying to dislodge the unwelcome fruit. The reptile was becoming very agitated, and Kirra was careful not to be raked by its dagger claws as she pulled Luke away to safety.

She lifted him up and sprinted toward the shade of the trees where her backpack was resting in the sand. Luke's tongue was hanging out of his mouth, and she knew that he needed water desperately. Just as they reached the trees, Matt and Sam ran up, sweaty and out of breath.

"We saw what happened! Is he okay?" asked Matt in a worried tone. He couldn't imagine a world without Luke in it.

"Help me cool him down, boys. Sam, take my wet scarf and lay it over his belly. One of you can fan him with this large leaf," Miss Kirra sat back on her heels and breathed deeply. She gently brushed away grains of sand that were clinging to his eyelashes and whiskers. Her lips were moving but no sound came out as she asked the spirits of the island to heal Luke.

Dad was halfway to the trees to check on Luke when he saw that Liam needed his help getting the helicopter ready to leave. He knew Luke and his sons were in good hands with Kirra, and the trees seemed to be a safer place for them than the open beach.

Liam and Dad removed the tie-downs from the rotors and walked around the outside of the chopper, looking for anything that would impede takeoff. They worked quickly, casting nervous glances at the Komodo thrashing around on the sand, its tail whipping back and forth.

"Is Luke going to be okay? Gosh, Kirra is one brave gal, the way she jumped on that Komodo and wedged the coconut in its mouth," Liam shook his head in admiration.

"She saved Luke's life, for sure," Dad said. "I haven't checked on him yet, but I'm hoping he's just shaken up a bit," Dad said. He noticed the heavy fire extinguisher at the pilot's feet and nodded his approval. "Good idea," he said as he tightened his grip on his spear and glanced down the beach.

The Komodo clan had indeed followed the Sawyers back but stopped short of actually reaching the helicopter. They were curious about the lizard who was still trying to dislodge the coconut from its mouth and formed a loose circle around it. The afflicted male began slamming its snout against the ground, and it was just a matter of time before the large nut was expelled.

With the outside preparations completed, Liam hopped into the pilot's seat and quickly went through the takeoff checklist. He made a circling motion with his finger to Dad, letting him know to step away once the blades starting spinning. Dad moved to a safe position and motioned to his family watching from the trees that it was time to board.

Everything seemed to happen at once. Miss Kirra emerged from the trees, carrying Luke in her arms, with Sam and Matt on either side of her. They protected their faces from the swirling sand and focused on getting to the helicopter as swiftly as they could.

POP! The coconut shot out of the Komodo's mouth like a hairy cannonball, hitting the sand and slowly rolling to a stop. The large male wasn't interested in the coconut any longer, stepping around it as he hastened toward the helicopter.

"Here they come!" shouted Matt. "Quick, Kirra, you and Luke get in the 'copter!"

Sam, Dad, and Matt stood shoulder to shoulder as Kirra hurried behind them to the open doorway. Liam was waiting and pulled her and Luke onboard.

The Komodos were rapidly closing in on the helicopter. The noise and wind produced by the spinning rotors didn't seem to be deterring them at all.

Dad picked up the fire extinguisher and removed the pin. "Matt, Sam, get inside! I got this!" He dropped to one knee as he squeezed the lever and slowly swept the tank from side to side. The foam spewed out about ten feet and the lizards stopped as their tongues flicked in and out trying to identify this strange, new scent.

Matt and Sam crouched beside their Dad and held their spears in front of them. "Should we try to board now, Dad?" Sam asked. "They're distracted by the foam."

Before Dad could answer, the Komodos began advancing toward them once again and the situation looked grim.

Matt tuned out all the commotion around him and remembered how renewed and grateful he had felt sitting in that geothermal pool. How he had felt the positive energy and love on this island. And suddenly he knew that his life journey wasn't ending today, not on this stretch of beach. That thought brought comfort, but how were they going to get out of this jam?

Matt saw movement at the edge of the rainforest. He squinted his eyes and nudged his brother. "What's moving over there?" he asked pointing to the trees.

"Monkeys!" they said in unison. GoMon was leading at least a dozen monkeys across the beach toward them. They didn't seem to be afraid of the helicopter either and chattered loudly as they approached the bank of Komodos. Some monkeys were holding rotten fruit or clumps of dried poop which they threw at the reptiles, darting away with mischievous looks on their faces as the lizards lunged at them.

Within minutes, the monkey troop had lured all the Komodos away from the helicopter and were a significant distance down the beach. Not one single monkey was caught by the reptiles, and they all disappeared, laughing, into the safety of the tall trees. Matt stood with his hand over his heart. "Thank you, GoMon, my friend," he whispered.

The Sawyers jumped into the copter, buckled their safety harnesses, and felt the island fall away as Captain Liam executed a smooth vertical takeoff. They were airborne!

Matt was relieved to see that Luke's eyes were open and he was looking around. Most importantly, he was drinking water from Miss Kirra's cupped hand and didn't appear to be in any pain. Matt looked back at Miss Kirra and thanked her for protecting Luke. She smiled and nodded her head.

"Thank goodness for GoMon and his friends, right?" she said to Matt and Sam.

"Yes, it was a marvelous monkey miracle!" Dad announced. "We'll be forever grateful to them."

Captain Liam made a banking turn away from the island and Matt had a strong desire to see it one last time. He twisted around in his seat.

"Miss Kirra, how do your people say *goodbye*?" he asked as he looked out the window at the island growing smaller and smaller.

"*Guwayu*," she replied. "We don't really have a word that means good-bye though. *Guwayu* means 'in a little while or later.'"

Everyone groaned. "Well, I don't plan on visiting the Isle of Tatsu 'later' so we can use our word *Hooroo*. And that's a firm goodbye," Matt laughed.

Epilogue

Six months after their return from the Isle of Tatsu found the Sawyer family embracing exciting new changes. There was reason to celebrate as the family welcomed a litter of Australian Shepherd puppies sired by Luke. He had completely recovered from his ordeal on the island and was a proud papa to six pups, three males and three females. Matt and Sam were allowed to keep one and they chose the smallest and prettiest one, naming her Luna.

They say what doesn't kill you makes you stronger, and Matt definitely was stronger, smarter, and kinder to himself and others after returning home from Tatsu. He realized that everyone has gifts, and life is about finding what makes you special and celebrating that. That's the message on his weekly vlog on a popular video sharing site that has thousands of loyal viewers. Sometimes he shares personal stories of struggles he's faced or demonstrates a cool survival tip.

Sam and Matt plan to join their Uncle Paul on an archaeological dig in Victoria. He is one of the paleontologists on site and got special permission for them to work on one of the most fascinating digs in years; namely, unearthing the rare skeleton of *Elaphrosaurus*. This Jurassic-period dinosaur was a relative of *T. Rex* but traded its early meat-eating diet for one of plants and was even known to range into southern polar lands.

It promises to be the trip of a lifetime, and Matt is counting down the days until they leave, eighty-eight to be precise. A perfect double even number.

Australian Slang

Ace - excellent, tops

Arvo - in the afternoon

Barbie - cooking on the grill

Biccy - cookies, for example Tim Tams

Brekky - breakfast

Cactus - dead or broken

Cuppa - a cup of tea

Devo - devastated

Dog's breakfast - very messy

Esky - a popular cooler

Fall off his perch - something or someone died

Fair-dinkum - good or genuine; excellent

Frog in a sock - to have lots of energy

Give it a burl - try it

G'day - popular greeting

Hooroo - word for goodbye

Heaps - very

Knackered - tired, exhausted

Mate - friend or pal

Salty - to be rude or angry about something

Shook - to be surprised

Tim Tams - a popular chocolate biscuit (cookie)

Vegemite - a salty, soft, dark brown spread usually eaten on bread

Woop woop - in the middle of nowhere

Glossary

Aft - toward the back of a ship

Aperture - an opening, hole, or gap

Antibiotics - medicine used to treat bacterial infections

Barometric pressure - the pressure of air pushing on Earth which is measured by a barometer

Barramundi - a delicious sport fish with a greenish bronze back and silvery sides found in seas from China to Australia

Beaufort Scale - Francis Beaufort, an officer of the Royal Navy, developed a scale in 1806 that compares conditions at sea using wind speed

Blue water sailing - this is an advanced type of sailing because you are on the open ocean for long periods of time

Bow - the forward part of a boat or ship

Burrow - a hole in the ground made by an animal for shelter

Camouflage – hiding something by covering it up or changing the way it looks

Charles Darwin - a British naturalist who suggested that when animals are best suited to their environment they will be the ones most likely to survive

Crater - a circular depression that occurs when a volcano ejects hot gases, rocks, and lava through naturally formed vents

Chronometer - a timepiece with a special mechanism for ensuring its accuracy, used for determining longitude at sea

Déjà vu - is a French phrase which means "already seen." It refers to the strange feeling people get when they are in a situation and feel like they've been there before but actually have not

Dinghy - a small boat, often used as a lifeboat and carried by a larger vessel

Doldrums - an area of the ocean near the equator where the seas and winds are very calm leaving ships stranded. The trade winds from the east and west meet here, which can cause brief, sudden storms to blow up occasionally

Drogue - a funnel-shaped canvas device trailed behind a boat on a long line and used for slowing the vessel down

Durian fruit - a large, tasty but foul-smelling fruit with a prickly rind

Epiphany - a sudden insight into the reality or meaning of something

Gale - a storm with winds of 34–47 knots (39–54 miles per hour)

Glade - an open grassy space in a forest

Hackles - the hairs that run along a dog's spine and stand up when the dog is excited, anxious, or aggressive

Halyard - a rope used for raising and lowering a sail on a ship

Head - bathroom on ships and boats

Geospirals - a concentration of energy in the Earth and often denoted by spiral drawings

Gunwale - the upper edge of the side of a boat or ship

Heave-to - setting the sails so that the mainsail wants to sail in one direction and the jib wants to sail in the opposite direction with the result of the boat standing nearly still

Helm - the wheel that controls the steering of a ship

Juju - an action or item that is believed to be harmful

Kapok tree - a tropical tree that has sharp prickles on its trunk and seed pods filled with fluffy fibers

Kilogram - metric unit of measurement. One kilogram is equal to 1000 grams. One kilogram is equal to 2.2 pounds. For example, 75 kilograms is equal to 165 pounds

Komodo dragon - the largest lizard in the reptile family and may reach a length of ten feet

Labyrinth - a place that has many confusing paths and passages

Latitude - these horizontal lines run north and south of the equator (0 degrees) and are part of a system used to pinpoint southern and northern locations on Earth

Ley Lines - straight lines of energy that crisscross the Earth and are dotted with sacred sites or natural landforms along them

Lizard brain – the oldest part of the brain that senses danger and where instincts like flight or fight reside

Longitude - these vertical lines run around the Earth beginning with the Prime Meridian in England (0 degrees) and are part of a system used to pinpoint eastern and western locations

Marina - a dock where boats are securely moored

Nautical - relates to ships, sailing, and navigation on the water

Navigate - this is how ships or aircraft find their way from one place to another

Nemesis - an opponent or rival that a person cannot overcome

Niche - an open, hollow space in a wall

Nocturnal - something that is active at night

Obsidian - a type of black or dark glass formed from cooling lava

Occam's Razor - A fourteenth century Franciscan friar stated that the simplest explanation for something is usually correct. He was an important philosopher in the Middle Ages

Outback – the remote central area of Australia, away from big cities

Port - the left-hand side of a boat when you are facing forward

Primordial - existing from an early time in history

Pyroclastic flow – extremely hot and fast flows of lava, ash, and gas during a volcanic eruption

Reefing - the act of making a sail smaller in response to increasing wind

Rudder - underwater blade at stern of boat that is turned horizontally to change the boat's direction

St. Elmo's Fire - a light appearing on tall objects like ship masts before or after storms. It is not lightning or fire but rather plasma being released from an electrical charge.

Satchel - small bag that is carried over your shoulder and used for carrying clothes, books, and other objects

Sextant - an older nautical instrument that sailors used to measure altitude of stars or the Sun and determines latitude and longitude

St. Christopher - patron saint of all travelers

Somnolent - sleepy, drowsy

Stalactites - pointy formations of minerals dissolved in dripping water that look like icicles hanging down from limestone cave ceilings

Starboard - the right-hand side of a boat when facing forward

Stern - the rear end of a ship or boat

Surveillance - the act of carefully watching something or someone

Tacking - basic sailing maneuver where a boat turns its bow toward the wind so that the direction from which the wind blows changes direction from one side to another

Talisman - an object believed to bring good luck, for example, a rabbit's foot

Tarpaulin - a large piece of waterproof material that is used to keeps things dry

Tatsu - Japanese word for dragon

Terrarium - a clear container used for growing plants or keeping small animals

Tourniquet - a bandage twisted tightly with a skinny device to slow or stop flow of bleeding

Venom - the poison secreted by some animals that is injected into prey by biting or stinging

Wahoo – a prized game fish found in tropical and subtropical waters